D0122634

FROGGED

FROGGED

Vivian Vande Velde

HARCOURT CHILDREN'S BOOKS
Houghton Mifflin Harcourt
Boston   New York

Harcourt Children's Books is an imprint of
Houghton Mifflin Harcourt Publishing Company.

www.hmhbooks.com

Text set in Goudy Old Style

Library of Congress Cataloging-in-Publication Data is available.
ISBN 978-0-547-94215-5

Manufactured in the United States of America
DOC 10 9 8 7 6 5 4 3
4500415376

To the handbell choir at St. Theodore's —
where we always like to announce
and celebrate good news

Contents

FROGGED

The Art of Being a Princess:
The Foreword

(Are you kidding? Nobody reads the foreword)

O ne should always strive," Princess Imogene read in *The Art of Being a Princess* (third revised edition), "to be the sort of princess about whom it is said: 'She was as good as she was beautiful.'"

"Ugh," Princess Imogene said. She slammed the book shut—hating it already, based on the first sentence. Hating the book, hating the writer, hating princesses in general, and most of all hating herself.

She suspected she was not as good as she could be, since parents, teachers, and assorted courtiers liked to point out that she was impatient, that she had a tendency to daydream, and that she was prone to ask "Why?" a bit more often, apparently, than was appropriate. She also knew she was not beautiful. Her own mother frequently assured her that *one day* she would be beautiful, that *one day* she would no longer be twelve and gawky, that *one day* she would fill in, blossom out, and grow into her body.

"Grow into my body?" Imogene had once made the mistake of echoing. "You make me sound like a tadpole or a caterpillar."

"Or a maggot," her little brother, Will, helpfully suggested with all of a seven-year-old boy's eagerness and tact.

Their mother, who was prone to sick headaches, had declared her need to lie down for a bit.

Imogene wondered if sick headaches were something *The Art of Being a Princess* encouraged. Or maybe that topic would be covered in *The Art of Being a Queen.*

As for future beauty, there was no way to know whether her mother's assurances about "someday" were based on something real her mother saw in her, or if, in fact, her mother was just being a mother.

So Imogene was neither as beautiful nor as good as a

princess should be, and therefore she found the book infuriating.

She was, however, good enough that she managed to resist her inclination to fling *The Art of Being a Princess* across her room. But she *did* toss it forcibly onto her bed, from which it bounced off, then skittered beneath.

The book had been a gift from her mother, in anticipation of Imogene's thirteenth birthday in another two weeks.

"If you start today and read a chapter a day," her mother had said this morning, with such bright optimism that Imogene couldn't help but suspect it had been practiced, "you'll have it finished the day before your birthday, and you'll be all ready."

Ready.

Meaning ready to be the sort of princess who didn't drop things, spill things, or trip over things. The sort of princess who always knew what to say and when not to say anything. The sort of princess who wasn't an embarrassment to her royal parents.

Imogene couldn't imagine why her mother thought two

weeks of reading would prepare her to be a proper princess when twelve years, eleven months, two weeks, and half a morning hadn't.

But her mother had looked so enthusiastic about the gift, so pleased with herself, so *hopeful,* that Imogene hadn't wanted to hurt her feelings. So she'd pretended interest by opening *The Art of Being a Princess* and looking over the table of contents. "Well," she'd said, forcing a little laugh, trying to find the humor in the situation, "twelve chapters in thirteen days: at least I get a day off for good behavior."

For a moment, her mother looked puzzled. Her expression moved close to the one that often came right before she announced having one of her headaches. Then she'd said, "The foreword, dear. Don't forget the foreword."

Ahh. The foreword. Imogene generally skipped over books' forewords, which were most often full of stuff too boring to put into the book itself, things like "This is the history of the entire known universe up until now . . ." And "These are the reasons why this book will be Good for You . . ." And "Thank you to my parents and my grandparents and my great-grandparents and my uncles and aunts and cousins and teachers and neighbors and the little girl who sat two rows over from me in the third grade . . ."

Maybe, Imogene thought, she could skip over the boring bits.

Mothers are legendary for being able to read the thoughts of their children at just the wrong moment. "You can read the foreword and then each chapter, one a day, in the morning, and then we can meet in the solarium for lunch together, just the two of us, and we can discuss any questions you might have."

"Wow," Imogene said. "That sounds like . . ." She couldn't come up with any word besides *torture*, and she knew better than to say that. She pasted a smile onto her face and nodded.

Apparently her mother's mind-reading ability had faded out by then. Either that or she, too, knew when not to say anything. In any case, she had leaned forward and given an air kiss in the vicinity of Imogene's cheek, then motioned one of her ladies in waiting to come over to discuss something-or-other, and Imogene had gone to her room.

First, Imogene had worked on the picture she'd been

drawing for the past week. It was the view out of her window: the castle courtyard, the stables across the way, the wall that surrounded the castle, the moat beyond, the trees forming the edge of the forest, the stream that came down from the hills that showed way off in the distance. The more she fiddled with the picture, the less pleased she was with her results, so she gave it up for fear she'd do something to ruin the whole thing.

Next she worked a bit on the dragon she was embroidering in the corner of a handkerchief for her brother, Will—embroidery being one of those princessly pursuits everyone seemed to favor and that Imogene actually enjoyed. Besides, Will, despite being a prince, was also a seven-year-old, and he really could use a handkerchief more often than he did. But today the thread seemed inclined to knot and break, and Imogene realized for the first time in a long while that she didn't so much enjoy doing the stitchery as having finished a project.

After that she found a chunk of bread in the pocket of the dress she'd been wearing yesterday, bread she'd intended to give to the wainwright's boy, who looked as though he didn't get enough to eat. But the bread had gone stale and had bits of lint stuck on it, so she decided to get another piece at lunch and meanwhile broke this one up and spread the crumbs out on the windowsill for the birds. Apparently the birds weren't interested today.

Imogene even considered taking a nap, except she really wasn't tired.

Which was how she came to be reading *The Art of Being a Princess*—the foreword.

Which started with that stupid line about how a princess should strive to be as good as she was beautiful.

"A princess can't help what she is or what she looks like," Imogene grumbled out loud to the book, as she fetched it back out from under the bed. Her hair, which she believed had more of a tendency to get mussed and tangled than anybody else's, got mussed and tangled.

She opened the book once more and thumbed through the pages. Her eye skimmed over paragraphs about girls with beautiful and elegant names, names like Sylvianna and Lilybelle and Esmeralda, and Adorabella.

Imogene had been named after her grandmothers, both of whom she loved dearly. They were two perfectly lovely ladies—who had perfectly awful names. Grandmother

Imogene was her father's mother, who had been named after *her* grandmother, so the name had already been almost a hundred years old-fashioned by the time Princess Imogene got it. And her mother's mother was Eustacia—who admitted she had no idea what her own parents were thinking when they named her.

It was a sad state of affairs, Princess Imogene Eustacia Wellington thought, when *Imogene* was the better of the two names you had to choose from.

Still, it was getting close to lunchtime, and it was no good saying this was a dull book told in a preachy, annoying style and that she wouldn't learn anything from it, but only be made to feel even more inadequate than she already did. So Imogene read the foreword, whose best quality was that it wasn't really as long as it *seemed* to be.

On her way to the solarium, Imogene worked out three things she could say, because she knew how discussions with her mother went. The queen would ask, as though it were a conversation, not a test, "Now, Imogene, tell me something you learned from your reading . . . Umm-hmm, and was there anything else . . . ? Very nice. And was that all?"

So Imogene would tell her:

1. *A princess should be as good as she is beautiful.*
2. *Being a princess is a duty and an honor.*
3.

Hmm . . .

3.

Well . . .

3. *A princess* . . .

No . . .

3.

Sigh. It had been such a boring foreword, and the thoughts on the page had already evaporated from her mind.

Imogene wondered if her mother would be paying

enough attention to notice if Imogene reworked number 1. Then it could be

1. *A princess should be as good as she is beautiful.*
2. *Being a princess is a duty and an honor.*
3. *A princess should be as beautiful as she is good.*

No. No matter how positive Imogene tried to be about her chances, she knew she probably wouldn't get away with that.

All right, then. She would divide number 2.

1. *A princess should be as good as she is beautiful.*
2. *Being a princess is a duty.*
3. *Being a princess is an honor.*

All right, then.

Imogene marched into the solarium and saw one of the ladies in waiting, not her mother.

"Oh, Princess Imogene," the lady said. "Your mother had to settle a dispute between two of the village women. She offers her apologies for disappointing you and said to assure you that she'll be happy to discuss *two* chapters with you tomorrow."

All that for nothing.

"Rats," Imogene said.

She was fairly certain that *The Art of Being a Princess* would disapprove.

Chapter 1

A Princess Is Always Kind and Helpful

*(Okay, but that doesn't mean she needs
to let people walk all over her)*

Princess Imogene considered going to her room to write down the three things she had learned from the foreword while she still remembered them.

That would be what a good princess would do, she told herself.

Then she told herself: *Fortunate thing for me that I'm only as good as I'm beautiful.*

Anyway, truly good and beautiful princesses could no doubt remember such things without having to take notes. They probably knew them without having to read them.

So, instead, Imogene headed toward the mill pond, which was her favorite relaxing place. She guessed that *The Art of Being a Princess* (third revised edition) probably had a whole chapter against princesses at mill ponds.

There were ducks and a pair of swans in the water, but they seemed to have an uncanny ability to know when she did—and when she did not—have bread in her pockets.

Imogene sat on the grassy bank and watched her fickle feathered friends gliding through the water.

Nobody has expectations for you, she thought.

Lucky things.

The sun was warm enough to make her comfortably drowsy, and she decided to lie down, even though her mother would fuss about grass stains. Imogene herself had low standards when it came to grass stains. Lying on her back made it easier to study the clouds drifting in the sky and to try to find ducks and geese and swans in them to mirror those in the water. But the best she could come up with was a shape that, sort of, looked like the back end of a dog, and another that could be a three-legged cow—if she tipped her head and squinted a bit.

From somewhere surprisingly close—surprising because she had not heard anyone approach—a small but gruff voice called: "Princess! Hey, Princess!"

Guiltily, Imogene jumped to her feet, convinced she was about to get reprimanded for lying down on the grass. But by whom? It was a male voice, and experience told her that most males—including her father—didn't seem as interested as the females of her acquaintance in what was and what was not proper princess-like behavior. Besides, this voice, despite being a bit gravelly, struck her as being somewhere between that of a child and that of an adult, so she expected to see someone close to her own age.

Except she saw no one.

"Hey!" the voice repeated. "Hey, Princess!"

The voice tickled at the edge of her memory, but she couldn't quite place it. And it struck her as being . . . well . . . a bit rude, even for a princess with low standards.

"Who are you?" she asked. "Where are you?"

"Here," the voice answered, zeroing in on the second question first. "Near your feet."

Near her feet was the tall grass and weeds at the water's edge, but that was indeed where the voice seemed to be coming from. Had someone swum across the pond? Except . . . the water here was too shallow—and too clogged with marsh weeds—to hide a person.

For a moment, her mind skittered to the ducks and swans, as though one of them had somehow gained the ability to speak—and to inquire why she hadn't brought food.

It was this momentary mental openness to a smaller-than-human speaker that made her notice the frog.

The frog bounced in place on a lily pad to make sure Imogene was looking at him. "Yeah, that's right," the frog said. "Me, over here."

"Wow," Princess Imogene said. "I mean . . . wow."

"Yeah, tell me about it," the frog croaked. "Mind coming down closer? It's hard for me to shout all the way up to you. I'm getting—you'll pardon the expression—a frog in my throat." The frog laughed, a mirthless, braying noise that Imogene couldn't help but think sounded more donkey than frog.

Still, she stepped forward and stooped down, even though her shoes squished in the mud and the edge of her dress dipped into the water.

"Whoa!" the frog said, taking a leap back to the next lily pad. "You got big feet there, Princess! Anybody ever tell you that you got big feet?"

Actually, her mother had bemoaned the fact that Imogene's feet weren't as dainty as they should be, but Imogene didn't think this was any of the frog's business. Instead, she said, "You're really talking? You, the frog?"

"A little slow on the uptake, aren't you, Princess? Yeah, sure, it's me talking. You see anybody else in, like, conversating distance? Sheesh!"

"Sorry," Imogene said. "It's just . . . you know . . . a bit unexpected."

"No kidding!" the frog croaked. "A day ago I was a prince, walking around on two legs. In my own kingdom, which is not this one, of course—though every bit as grand, if I do say so myself. So there I was, as happy as a clam—though maybe under the circumstances I shouldn't mix my whatta-you-call-'ems?—animal metaphones."

"Metaphors," Imogene corrected.

"Yeah, whatever, Little Princess Know-It-All," the frog said. "For someone who's so smart, you never heard of a prince what gets himself in trouble—through no fault of his own, I might add—with a witch what goes and changes him into a frog?"

"Well, yes," Imogene admitted, "though I've never personally met either a wi—"

"Ta-dah!" the frog interrupted, holding his little frog arms out expansively.

"Where did you say you're from?" Imogene asked.

"Different kingdom," the frog said. "Not this one."

"Yes, I understand," she said. "But what's the name of your kingdom? I'm just wondering if it's someplace I've heard my father mention—if he knows your father."

"Oh," the frog said. "Not likely. It's a small kingdom. We're north of here." Before Imogene could do more than open her mouth, he added, "Well, sort of north-ish. By way of east-northwest. Anyway, it's very small. You wouldn't of ever heard of us."

"I see," said Princess Imogene, not wanting to be discourteous, even though it all seemed very strange. "It's only that you don't sound very much like the other princes I've met."

"Oh, that's very nice!" the frog snapped. "Make fun of my accent."

"No, it's not so much an accent—"

"And of the fact that I sound like a frog. Come on, Princess, keep up! Weren't you listening to the whole the-witch-changed-me-into-a-frog part? This is the way frogs talk, except you never noticed before on account of you not being a frog and all."

It made sense. Sort of. Imogene supposed.

"So, you going to help me out, Princess?" the frog asked.

"Help you out?" Imogene repeated.

The frog sighed. "You aren't very well-read for a princess, are you, Princess? A witch puts a spell on a prince, turns the prince into a frog, the only way to break the spell is if a princess comes along and . . . you know . . ." The frog puckered his lips.

"Oh." Imogene could feel her face begin to flush. "I've never kissed a boy," she admitted, figuring that kissing her little brother Will on the cheek or forehead didn't count.

"Hello!" the frog said. "I'm not a boy. I'm a frog. Who used to be a prince. Princess, you got to pay attention."

"I am," Imogene told him, beginning to feel miffed at the frog's attitude. But she didn't want to sound snooty or overly suspicious, like her mother. "It's just this is all new to me."

"Well, yeah!" the frog said. "Think how I feel about it!"

And it was by doing exactly that—thinking how the prince-turned-frog must feel—that Imogene decided to help him.

"All right," she said, "how do we do this?"

The frog rolled his eyes, which is not a pretty sight in a frog. "Well, it seems to me that either the lips gotta come down to the frog, or the frog's gotta go up to the lips."

Imogene considered. Though the hem of her dress was already thoroughly wet, she didn't want to sit or kneel on the soggy ground. But she didn't relish the idea of picking up the frog, which seemed much more her brother Will's type of interest. Besides, she didn't know how this kissing-a-frog-back-into-a-prince thing worked. Would he *instantly* resume his human form? While she was holding him?

As she was weighing her options, the frog said, "Don't worry, Princess: I got my clothes on. They changed right along with me."

"Oh my!" said Imogene, who hadn't even thought to

worry about *that*. Eager to get this over with, she decided to kneel down after all, which entirely soaked the bottom half of her dress before she thought that what she *should* have done was ask the frog to hop to higher ground with her.

Too late now. She bent all the way down, stretched her neck forward, puckered her lips, and—at the last moment—closed her eyes.

Something cold and slightly spinach-y touched her lips. Imogene forced herself not to shudder, forced herself to kiss.

She hadn't been favorably impressed with the frog, but a tingly sensation washed over her entire body, so she told herself maybe it was true love after all. She rather hoped not, but she'd read about such things.

Except . . . except that the tingling didn't stop when the kiss did. It escalated. She was willing to accept the dizziness, but her body became downright fizzy. Her skin tickled and prickled. *This is what a gherkin must feel like*, she thought, *when it picklefies*. She couldn't recall a single book or love ballad she'd ever heard mentioning such a sensation.

Imogene opened her eyes, and the dizziness doubled, tripled, quadrupled. The world tipped and broke into little pieces, then reassembled itself differently, reminding her of the time she had looked through the wrong end of her father's telescope.

She quickly closed her eyes again, squeezing them tightly to keep that disorienting world out.

"Princess?"

Imogene wondered if the frog prince was experiencing the same effects.

"Princess, you all right?"

Except his voice sounded much steadier than she felt.

And loud.

And high up.

It must have worked, she thought. He'd turned back into a person, and he was standing up over her, while she still knelt in the mucky weeds.

"I'm sorry, Princess," the frog prince said. "It was the only way to take the spell off of me."

Sorry didn't sound good.

Imogene opened her eyes, and the world once more shifted a bit, then settled.

The prince—Imogene didn't like to think of herself as a snob, but she thought he had a very shabby appearance for a prince, even for one just recently rescued from frog-hood—the prince absolutely loomed over her.

More oddly, so did the marsh grass.

Imogene looked down to the ground—which was a lot closer to her than she'd have expected.

That was when she saw her skinny green legs. And her webbed feet.

A startled "Rrrribitt" escaped from her mouth.

And that was how Princess Imogene Eustacia Wellington became a frog.

Chapter 2

A Princess Should Be a Good Listener

(Of course, "good" doesn't mean she should believe everything she hears)

Princess Imogene glared at the boy who had formerly been a frog, the boy who had never been a prince—the boy who was, in fact, the son of the wagon maker, the wainwright's boy. "Did you know that was going to happen?" she demanded. Her voice was small and a bit croaky, just as his had been, back when he'd been a frog.

"What?" the boy asked—difficult to tell if he was going for innocent or dimwitted. Neither was believable. By the way he wouldn't meet her gaze, she saw that he knew exactly what she was talking about.

"That wasn't very nice," she told him. Even as she said

it, she thought it was perhaps the biggest understatement of the world.

But he only shrugged. Which was pretty halfhearted if meant as an acknowledgment, and woefully inadequate as an apology.

"How do I turn back to myself?"

Again the shrug.

And—once again—she suspected she already had the answer. She just didn't like it. "I have to get somebody else to kiss me," she said, not even asking, "and then that person will become a frog in my place."

For such a talkative frog, the boy now seemed beyond communicating except through lifting and dropping his shoulders.

"Well, that's just . . . just . . ." In her agitation, another "Rrr-bitt" escaped from her little green lips. "Well it goes beyond *mean*. I could never do that to someone."

And yet if she didn't, would she stay a frog?

Forever?

Surely there had to be another way.

Didn't there?

The boy gave another silent shoulderly answer.

But after a moment, he suggested, "Maybe you could choose someone you don't like, someone who"—again with a shrug—"deserves it. Then it might not be so bad."

"Excuse me," Imogene said, drawing herself up to her full two and a half inches. "You're saying you don't like me? You're saying I *deserved* to be turned into a frog?"

"You were here," the boy told her, which was not exactly a strong affirmation of his high regard for her.

"But you chose to use me," Imogene said. What was she hoping for? He'd already apologized. Sort of. As much, she suspected, as he ever would.

The boy said, "Look, Princess, you're a princess. You always got good things your whole life. Me, I got a father what smacks me on the side of the head when he thinks I'm not working hard enough. And more squalling brothers and sisters than it's fair for any one boy to have to deal with. And a ma what's too tired to keep up with 'em."

Never mind, Princess Imogene thought, feeling just the slightest bit sorry for herself, *that I saw all that and tried to help.*

But before she could decide if she should remind him that she sometimes brought bread for him to eat, he finished, "Maybe it was my turn to have a little bit of luck."

Luck, Imogene thought. It was just her *bad* luck that she'd come here.

"Well, I gotta go, Princess," the boy said. "I already been gone overnight, and my father is like to be really mad."

"Ribbit!" Imogene called as he turned from her. She quickly managed to come back to human speech. "Wait!" Then, because

1. she had been raised to always remember her manners, but mostly because
2. he'd clearly indicated he resented her being a princess,

she added, "Please."

He stopped but didn't turn to face her. "You don't even know my name," he pointed out. "Here you go, wanting to call me back, but you don't know how except as"—he slipped into a la-di-da voice that she could only assume was supposed to sound like hers—"that-poor-boy-I'm-oh-so-kind-enough-to-help."

So, Imogene thought, it was a good thing she hadn't mentioned the bread before.

"I'm sorry," she said.

He had turned *her* into a frog, and she was apologizing.

But still. "I'm sorry I never asked your name."

Finally, sulkily, the boy faced her. "Harry," the boy told her. "My name is Harry."

Before he could turn around for good and walk away, she hurriedly said, "Hello, Harry. I'm Imogene."

He snorted, which might have meant he thought that was obvious. Or maybe it meant he thought she was talking down to him by not saying, "Princess Imogene." But they both knew what she was.

And what he was.

She said, "Please, Harry, will you tell me what happened?" Then, seeing the I-can't-believe-you're-asking-me-that expression on his face, she clarified, "To you. How did *you* get changed into a frog?"

But even that question seemed to try his patience. "I done told you," he said. "You try to act like you're a regular person, but you don't listen. I already said."

And with that, he did resume walking away.

"A witch!" Imogene called after him. She started jumping, following as he strode through the grass that separated the mill pond from the road, but she quickly saw she could never catch up. Her frog legs were strong for jumping both high and long, but not so good for a whole bunch of jumps, one right after another. "I *was* listening. I *did* hear you. You said a witch turned you into a frog, and you said she did it for no reason." She didn't point out that he had also said he was a prince, so he was perhaps not the most reliable person from whom to be getting her information. She finished all in a rush and raised her voice, because the distance between them was growing and he gave no sign that he intended to stop. "But you didn't give me the specifics."

"Specifics," he muttered, still striding away from her. But then he did finally face her again, though he continued walking—more slowly—backwards. "Specifics."

The way he lingered over the word made Imogene suspect that he might not know what it meant, but that he didn't want to admit so. He *had* tried to bluff his way through "metaphor." But he had also sort of gotten it. She said, "Who the witch was. Where the two of you crossed paths. What you were doing when—for no reason—she put the spell on you." It couldn't hurt to take his side. "If she said anything to you. That kind of specifics."

She had time for all this because he had stopped walking and she'd had the chance to close some of the distance between them. She was, however, panting from all the jumping, which was harder work than she would have ever thought. Not that she had ever thought about any of it: jumping or frogs or jumping frogs.

Luckily, he answered—luckily because she didn't have breath for any more questions *or* jumps.

"She's the old lady what lives in the house down the way from where my friend Tolf lives, you know, the house behind where the cooper has his shop?"

Imogene managed to croak out, "*Who* lives behind the cooper's shop: Tolf or the old lady?"

Harry rolled his eyes. "Tolf. The witch's house is down the way from him. But before you get to the blacksmith's shop. She has apple trees in her yard. More apple trees—more apples—than anyone could ever use."

Imogene had a suspicion she could guess where this story was going, but she nodded to encourage him.

Harry said, "I heard tell she was a witch, but I figured that was talk she started herself, so as to keep people from pestering her. Either that, or people call her witch causin' she's as ugly as the wrong end of a wild pig."

Imogene didn't interrupt to ask him *which* was the wrong end of a wild pig. That is, she supposed she knew, but she wasn't sure, since she wouldn't want to come face to face with either end. And the end that, technically speaking, had a face to come face to face with had nasty sharp tusks, and surely those were something most anyone would want to avoid.

Her own parents didn't believe in witches, not outside of stories, and they certainly didn't believe in name-calling those who were unfortunate in their physical appearance.

But before she could become too distracted by either of those lines of thinking, Harry finished, "And, I mean, if you were a witch what knew spells, wouldn't the first spell you cast be to improve your looks from ugly to at least passable?"

"Yes," Imogene said, because what instantly came to mind was all those princesses who were as good as they were beautiful, and she'd always wanted that. Well, truth be told: she was more interested in the beautiful part than the good part. But then she said, "Well, no, probably it would be the second thing I'd wish for." Because—as nice as it would be to be beautiful—it was more important to be healthy and of sound body. As someone who had just had her body changed into that of a frog, she knew the importance of this. But that was selfish, because of course she'd also want her family to be healthy, so she amended her statement to "Well, actually the third." Her mind kept spinning and bouncing off different possibilities. "Or, no, wait a minute: the fourth, because— Except . . . Maybe the fifth . . . Unless it was the sixth. Or it could be—"

"Princess," Harry interrupted firmly, and even a bit crankily for all her dithering.

"What?"

"It would be one of the first."

She pondered that, weighing it.

"If you were a witch?" Harry sounded exasperated. "With lots of years to cast lots of spells?"

"But isn't that the point?" Imogene said. "She *did* turn out to be a witch. Who hasn't made herself attractive. For whatever reason."

"You always got to be right, don't you, Princess?" Harry snapped.

"You're the one who brought it up," Imogene snapped right back.

"Anyways," Harry said, "I didn't believe she was a witch, even though *you* probably would of on account of you being a princess and being so smart about everything. And there was her yard, with all them apples nobody was eating except for the worms once them apples fell off them trees, and with me with never enough to eat."

"So you went into her yard?" Imogene said. "To take an apple because you were hungry? And she caught you and changed you into a frog for *that?*" It hardly seemed fair.

Harry squirmed. "Well," he admitted, "with me and my brothers and sisters with never enough to eat."

"All right," Imogene said. "So you took . . . several . . . apples? For your brothers and sisters?" She thought there might be six of the children, total, but she wasn't absolutely certain.

It was hard to believe someone could be so cruel to begrudge six—or even seven—hungry children an apple each, and Imogene took a few moments to think about going to someone like that and asking for help in de-frogging herself.

Moments Harry apparently spent thinking about something, too.

"Well . . ." he said.

That brought her back quickly. "What?"

"A few of them apples—you, know, the ones on the ground—they were wormy. And mushy. They were no good to eat."

Imogene tapped her little webbed foot. "And so?" she prompted.

"So," Harry admitted, "I threw a few of them, for target practice."

"*Target practice?*" Imogene demanded. "Don't tell me you were throwing apples at the witch."

"No!" Harry assured her. "I'd never do that." His squirming resumed. "Not intentionally." He sighed, as though she was interrogating him. "All right, all right, I was throwing them at her door. How was I to know she was home? How was I to know she'd choose *then* to come out?"

Imogene sighed, too. "And that was when she turned you into a frog? After you accidentally hit her with an apple?"

Harry considered for a bit too long before saying, "More or less."

"More or less what?" Imogene snapped.

"I was throwing the apples fast," Harry said. "And I'm a very good shot. Maybe two hit her."

Imogene just looked at him and waited.

"Three at the most."

"Anything else you need to tell me?"

"No, Princess, that's about it. What do you need to know all this for, anyway?"

It was so obvious, Imogene couldn't believe he had to ask. "So I can track her down. And convince her to take the spell off me without my having to pass it on to someone else."

Harry snorted. "Yeah, well—good luck with that!" he said.

Chapter 3

A Princess Ought to Be Fearless

*(That's just crazy: the only people who are fearless
are people who have no imagination)*

Princess Imogene had hoped that Harry would come
with her. But the way he wished her good luck *sounded*
like the end of the conversation.

And the way he turned around and walked away *looked*
like the end of the conversation.

"Aren't you going to help me?" she called after him.

"Nope," he called back.

And that most certainly *was* the end of the conversation.

Not sure how far her croaky little voice would carry, she
shouted after him, "You could at least bring me there." He
couldn't hear her, not at that distance, but it was hard to

give up. "Just to the edge of her property. Even if . . ." He'd reached the top of the little hill. Well, it was really more of an incline than a hill; it only looked like a hill to someone who was just two and a half inches tall. But in any case, Harry reached the road that led to the mill itself, and he disappeared beyond the corner of the building with never a glance backwards. Her voice dropped to a mutter, and she finished, "Even if you're too afraid to face her again."

Imogene sighed.

Well, she would just have to *not* be afraid. She would have to get there on her own.

Imogene began jumping. And jumping. And jumping.

A pesky gnat made a nuisance of itself by circling her head.

Imogene fully intended to swat it away, but instead of her hand coming up, her mouth opened and her tongue shot out.

"*Ech!*" She tried to cough the bug out of her throat, but her throat did the exact opposite of what she wanted—and she swallowed it instead.

"*Ech! Ech! Ech!*" But it wouldn't come back up.

She tried to convince herself that so long as she was a

frog, eating a gnat was the same as eating peaches in cream was for her princess self.

But she wasn't that easy to fool.

Just never mind, she reflected, even though she was still fighting not to gag. *The best thing you can do is to turn back to your princess self as quickly as possible.*

And the best way to do that was to confront the witch as quickly as possible.

Surely, Imogene theorized, the witch would have to listen to good sense and agree that there was no reason *Imogene* should suffer for what the wainwright's boy had done.

But, again, Imogene wasn't that easy to fool.

Still, she jumped up the grassy incline that had become a hill and estimated that was about a tenth of the way she had to go. She might have to take a few rests as she traveled, but this was certainly doable.

She jumped onto the road, since that—being more level than the grassy slope—should be easier.

Her big froggy eyes caught a movement off to the side, and she hopped back just in time to avoid being run over by the wheel of the cart that the greengrocer was pushing.

Not becoming a froggy slick on the road would have been

indisputably a good thing if only she hadn't landed on top of the bare foot of the greengrocer's daughter, a five-year-old who was walking behind and off to the side of the cart and who apparently didn't like frogs. Or, at least, didn't like frogs unexpectedly landing on her.

The girl screamed—which Imogene thought was an over-reaction no matter how you looked at it—and kicked her foot up into the air, which flung Imogene back into the grass from which she'd just come.

The good news was that Imogene landed on something soft.

The bad news was that she landed on something furry.

The *really* bad news was that the soft, furry thing she'd landed on was a big orange cat. And the way it was crouched where road met grass—right where Imogene had come out from not more than a jump, a scream, and a kick away—suggested that the cat had, in fact, been stalking her.

Who could have guessed that such a fat old cat with a frog sitting on its head could move so fast? Or so nimbly?

First, it jumped straight up into the air as though it, too, had a bit of frog in its makeup.

With no better plan than not to fall off, Imogene dug her green webbed toes into the orange fur.

Then, the cat tried to twist itself to get its mouth over to the back of its head.

With no better plan than not to get eaten, Imogene hunkered down where she was, which seemed as though it had to be the most difficult place for the cat to reach.

Finally, the cat threw itself into the dust of the road and rolled.

Too dizzy to have any plan at all, Imogene fell off.

The cat jumped to its feet.

Imogene tried to jump to hers, too, but apparently frogs get dizzy faster than cats. Or, in any case, their dizziness lasts longer. Whatever the reason, her legs wobbled and buckled beneath her, while the cat—all fluffed out, stiff-legged, and spitting—advanced on her.

"Mad cat!" the greengrocer shouted, stepping between his small daughter and the cat that looked about to attack her—if you hadn't noticed the frog that the cat had been working to dislodge, the frog who now was too feeble to jump to safety. "Move, Astrid!" the greengrocer commanded, shoving his half-shrieking, half-sobbing daughter out of what must have looked to him to be harm's way. He reached into his cart to find a weapon amongst the produce he hadn't been able to sell after a morning at the market: two or three wilted heads of lettuce, a small pile of mostly limp carrots, the onion—split now—that had rolled around loose in the cart but was too far for him to reach. Instead, he pulled up the bucket of water in which he'd had radishes soaking, and flung the water—leftover radishes and all—at the cat.

Apparently the cat didn't like having water dumped on it even more than it didn't like having a frog land on it.

With an angry yowl, the cat ran off, which was a good thing for Imogene, because one of the radishes had bonked her on the head, so that now she was not only dizzy, but she had a headache, and she was less likely than ever to be able to jump out of the radish-water puddle and into the grass.

"Did that nasty old cat hurt you?" the greengrocer asked.

Imogene was about to answer, *No, but thank you for asking,* when she realized the man was kneeling in front of his daughter, speaking to her.

The girl was sobbing—as though *she* had ever been in

danger—but managed to get out, "Not the cat. The *frog* tried to bite me."

Imogene could have denied the accusation, but she doubted a talking frog would help the situation. Besides, even if she was able to convince these two that she was, in fact, Princess Imogene froggified and should be returned home, what would that accomplish? Her mother would no doubt get one of the very worst of her headaches and have to go to bed for at least two days. Her father would put on a brave face—as king, he'd have to—but he, also, would be sick with worry. And even with all that, what could they actually do? Would they be any likelier than Imogene herself to be able to talk the witch into reversing her spell? Either the witch would be reasonable, or she would not. Imogene had read enough fairy tales to worry that a royal decree on the matter was less likely to soften the witch's heart and more likely to make her stubborn.

Imogene watched the greengrocer pick up his daughter. He set her down to ride in the cart, her legs swinging over the back edge, near where he would stand when he was pushing the cart, so he could keep an eye on her safety. "There, there," he said. "Frogs don't bite."

"Jumped on me," the girl insisted.

"Did it?" the greengrocer said with exaggerated enthusiasm. Lifting up the handles of the cart, he resumed pushing. "That's considered great good luck, you know, to have a frog land on you."

"It is?" the girl asked, calming down to a sniffle.

The two of them passed beyond Imogene's hearing while the greengrocer was asserting that being frog-jumped was one of the luckiest things in the world, right up there with rain on your wedding day. This was so like Imogene's own father, who was always making up similar nonsensical things to cheer up his children, that Imogene took a moment to reconsider her decision about whether to go home to get her parents' help.

But the sticking point was that bit about going *home*. If, by making it from the pond to the road, Imogene had traveled a tenth of the way to the witch's house, that meant she had traveled about a forty-fifth of the way back to the castle. Too many chances to get stepped on, Imogene thought. Or eaten. Or squished by a cart wheel. And, yes, she might be able to ask someone for help. But then she'd have to worry about how people might react to her saying, "Hello. I may look like a frog, but, really, I'm Princess Imogene. Please carry me back to the castle, and I'm sure my parents will give you a token of their appreciation for your trouble." What if she got swatted before she could get all that out?

See the witch first, Imogene told herself. *If that doesn't work out, THEN you can worry about what to do next.*

And so Imogene jumped and jumped and jumped . . .

. . . and jumped and jumped and jumped . . .

. . . and jumped and jumped and jumped some more.

If she saw somebody coming, she jumped off the road so as to avoid their big feet. (Her mother thought *she* had big feet? *Everybody's* feet look big when you're a frog.) Once, when the somebody coming was a dog, Imogene had to jump farther off the road, into a pile of firewood stacked in someone's yard. The dog came to investigate and poked its paw into the spaces between the wood, trying to get at Imogene, but fortunately it barked in its excitement, and the homeowner came out and shooed it away.

By then, Imogene's head felt ready to split open. She hadn't had many headaches in her life, but this one made her a little more sympathetic toward her mother's inclination to take to bed with hers. Who could have guessed being rolled over by a cat and getting hit on the head with a radish and jump-jump-jumping toward a witch's house could make someone feel so miserable? The dizziness had come back, and Imogene was convinced she was doubling the distance she had to travel by no longer being able to jump in a straight line. If another person—or another dog, cat, cart, or radish—came down the road, would she ever be able to get away? And even when a fly buzzed her, she was too tired to shoot her tongue out to get it, which she didn't know whether to take as a good thing or bad. Her tongue felt as big and dry and unmovable as a tree root in her mouth. She forced herself to keep jumping because she feared that if she stopped, she'd never be able to start again.

But eventually she realized that the pounding in her ears wasn't totally because of the headache; part of it was actually hearing the blacksmith at work in his shop at the end of the street, pounding a piece of metal on his anvil.

Before you get to the blacksmith's shop, Harry had said. That was where the witch lived. And, sure enough, two houses before the smithy was a neat little cottage with three scrawny apple trees in the yard. From the way Harry had talked about her having so very many apples, Imogene had thought the witch must have an orchard in her yard. But Imogene hadn't passed in front of another house with any apple trees at all—or at least she didn't think she had. Surely, as distracting as her aching head was, she would have noticed. This must be it: the house where the witch lived.

So Imogene had arrived—which was, of course, what she'd wanted. But it was still scary. Tottering with exhaustion, she jumped into the yard, up to the front door . . .

And then she had no idea what to do.

"Hello," she called. "Anybody home?" But her tired frog voice was no louder than a demure princess whisper. *Mother would be so pleased,* Imogene thought, because her mother was always reminding her to use her in-castle voice.

Imogene no longer had hands with knuckles for rapping, and frogs' legs aren't made for kicking at doors.

Loud as she could, she once again croaked, "Is anyone home?"

After all that, no one answered.

Maybe, Imogene thought, the witch was in her backyard.

Fighting the inclination to remain where she was and to wait for the witch to find her—which would be by far the easiest thing to do—Imogene forced herself to jump around to the backyard. There was a little well here and an herb garden and more trees: cherry and peach and what might have been a pear, but no more apple trees. *Still, I imagine keeping the village boys out of the fruit trees must be a constant chore for her,* Imogene thought. *No wonder she sometimes gets cranky.*

Imogene's headache must have made her not so observant as she should have been, for only after noticing all those other features of the backyard did she see the witch. She was sitting on a chair in the shade of one of the peach trees, reading a book.

The Art of Being a Witch? Imogene wondered.

The woman was not so ugly as Harry had led her to believe. Just wrinkled, like Imogene's grandmothers. And with hair that—although white—looked as hard to control as Imogene's own. So, all in all, with her feet up on an embroidered stool and a cup of tea resting on a tree stump by her elbow, the witch looked friendlier than Imogene had dared to hope.

Imogene jumped closer, although her head was swimming and her muscles ached, and she trembled so badly that she actually tipped over on her last couple of landings.

The witch must have seen her out of the corner of her eye, for she was looking up from her book when Imogene addressed her. "Hello," Imogene said, deciding one could never go wrong with good manners. Her voice was even croakier than usual. "I'm sorry to interrupt you, but—"

The witch threw the book aside without even closing it and jumped to her feet. Then she scooped Imogene up in her hand and flung her into the well.

Chapter 4

A Princess Should Be Quick-Witted

(EVERYBODY should be quick-witted)

The water closed over Imogene's head.

I'm going to die, Imogene thought, for she didn't know how to swim.

Her brother, Will, despite being five years younger, already knew how to swim. But of course swimming was yet another of those things that princesses — or even ladies — just didn't do.

Dying, alone — thanks to being flung into a well by a witch who hadn't even waited to hear what she'd come to say — was bad enough. Making things even worse was the knowledge that her parents would never know what had happened to her. At first, Mother would be annoyed when Imogene didn't return home by late afternoon, and she would probably start practicing her reprimand—Imogene was sure her mother kept a list of motherly complaints and chastisements that she would periodically read over and rehearse in order to be prepared for whatever Imogene did wrong. But as afternoon turned to evening, both Mother and Father would shift to worry—worry that would become more and more frantic as the evening started to grow dark. Footmen and guards and servants would be sent out looking for her, through the night . . .

. . . the next day . . .

. . . the next weeks . . .

. . . and all the while they would never learn a hint about what had happened to her.

Harry the wainwright's boy, of course, could not tell what he knew and what he might surmise—not without getting blamed for what he had done. Imogene was fairly certain that, if questioned, he could be counted on to say, "What? Who? Where would I ever get the chance to see someone the likes of her?"

Would the witch begin to suspect that the talking frog

she had tossed into the well might be the missing princess? Imogene wondered if the witch would feel bad *then*.

Probably not. She was, after all, a witch.

Then again, Imogene realized that she was having a lot of time for all these thoughts and wonderings.

She opened her eyes, which she had closed when she'd hit the water. She'd floated up to the water's surface, her little frog body buoyant, and her little frog legs were instinctively moving her in circles.

Oh, she thought, *that's right. FROGS don't have to wait for their mothers to give permission for swimming lessons.*

Imogene floundered for a second as she thought too much and her human brain made her frog body forget what it knew.

A hand reached into the water and supported her.

A gnarled, old woman's hand.

A witch's hand.

In that moment, Imogene realized that she hadn't even been in the well itself; she'd been in the well's bucket. And the bucket was resting near the surface.

The witch was looking at her with what could almost pass as concern and gently asked, "Are you all right?"

And Imogene realized her headache was gone, her aching muscles were no longer trembling with exhaustion, and she felt, in fact, fine.

"Yes," she answered with surprise.

Like Imogene's mother, the witch could evidently change moods at a moment's notice. The quiet worry on her face shifted into that same I-can't-believe-you'd-do-such-a-foolish-thing look that was, again, very like Imogene's mother.

"Frogs," the witch said, "are amphibious. You need water. You can't go traipsing around on dry land the same as you could do as a person. Didn't you wonder why you couldn't even hop straight? What were you thinking?"

"I'm sorry," Imogene said, even as she realized this was the second time this afternoon that she was apologizing to someone who, if you looked at the situation only slightly differently, might be expected to apologize to *her*. She added, "I guess I was thinking like a princess instead of like a frog." She didn't know if the witch recognized her in all her greenness, and just in case she didn't, Imogene thought it might be useful for the witch to know that this particular girl-turned-frog was somebody important. Or at least someone with important parents. Parents who would come looking for her. Which meant it might be safest and best for everyone for the witch to just go ahead and turn Imogene back into a girl now.

Obviously not nearly so awed or intimidated as Imogene had hoped, the witch set her down in the grass and said, "So, now you know. Stick to where it's wet."

The witch went back to her chair and resumed reading.

Had she not heard the part where Imogene had said she was a princess?

"Excuse me . . ." Imogene said.

"All right," the witch said, never glancing up from her book.

Imogene sighed impatiently. "No," she said more forcefully, "I mean: Excuse me."

Still not glancing up from her book, the witch took a sip of her tea and said, "Really. Think nothing of it. Accidents happen. I'm glad I was here to help."

Imogene jumped to directly in front of the chair and cleared her throat. Which is pretty impressive when a frog does it.

The witch didn't seem to notice.

Not being noticed was something Imogene could fix. With her renewed vigor, she jumped onto the book.

"Hey!" the witch said. "Your feet are wet!"

"I'm a frog," Imogene reminded her.

"You're a frog who's leaving wet footprints on my book."

"Well," Imogene pointed out, her patience having snapped, "I wouldn't be able to do that if I was, for example, *back in my princess shape.*"

"Probably not," the witch agreed. "Unless it was a very big book."

Imogene frequently found it difficult to talk to adults, but this witch was impossible.

And yet the witch slid a hand beneath Imogene's feet to protect the book, but she didn't toss Imogene back into the well, or anywhere else for that matter. Instead, she continued to sit with a patience—or at least a stillness—that seemed to be a sign that she was willing to listen.

Imogene asked, "Do you have any idea who I am?"

"You indicated that you were a princess," the witch said, "though, of course, I have no way of knowing if that's true."

"As a matter of fact," Imogene said, "speaking of things

true and not true . . . I'm the princess who kissed the wainwright's boy *you* turned into a frog, and *he* lied to me."

The witch's brow furrowed as she tried to work this out. "Did you kiss him before I turned him into a frog or after?"

"Af—" Imogene started to say, but she interrupted herself to go *"Eww!"* and then again *"Eww!"* before she finished with "After." Then she added another *"Eww."*

"All right," the witch said. "And your point—beyond *Eww!*—is . . . ?"

"He told me he was a prince," Imogene explained, "and that I needed to kiss him for him to turn back into a prince."

"You're a very gullible princess," the witch said.

Imogene stamped one of her little green feet in frustration for how this conversation was going.

The witch asked, "So, is the *Eww!* for him being a wainwright's boy and not a prince? Making you not only gullible, but stuck-up?"

Stuck-up was the way Imogene thought her mother acted, and she hated to be compared to her. "The *Eww!*" she protested, "is because I'm only twelve. Well, almost thirteen, but not for another two weeks. But still, I don't kiss boys.

Well, once, when we were both five, I kissed Prince Malcolm, who's the son of my father's best friend, King Calum. But our parents made us do it, because we hardly ever see them since they live so far away, and all the grownups were kissing one another to say goodbye when they were returning home, and they made us."

"Twelve *is* very young," the witch agreed wistfully. "I can almost remember being twelve myself . . ." She looked as though she was beginning to drift off into a pleasant daydream.

"But what I'm saying," Imogene said, rather loudly, to bring the witch back out of her memories, "is that you turned the wainwright's boy into a frog, for stealing apples for himself and his hungry brothers and sisters—he admitted to me afterward—and for throwing apples at your front door, and, yes, he did tell me that one of them accidentally hit you . . ."

"Gullible," the witch accused Imogene once again. "He is the ringleader of a group of boys who have come here just about every day this summer. They take the fruit off the trees, which is something they'd be welcome to if they ate them. But mostly they use them to have battles, hurling them at each other and at my house. They climb the trees and break the branches; they trample my herb garden; they throw old shoes down my well. Yesterday I'd had my fill."

"Oh," Imogene said. She should have guessed from the way Harry had been so reluctant to share the story that he had not told her the half of it. "I am truly sorry they've been tormenting you."

The witch said, "Well, at least you *are* more polite than they are."

Which gave Imogene the courage to say, "So, he did what he did, you did what you did—and I'm not saying you were wrong to get annoyed at him—but then all I did was to feel sorry for this poor little frog who told me he hadn't done anything wrong, and that he needed me to kiss him back into human shape. And he didn't warn me I would become a frog in his place."

"Hmm," the witch said. "Does that mean you wouldn't have helped him if you had known it would cost you?"

"I—I don't know," Imogene stammered. She thought about it for several seconds. All the while, the witch didn't say anything. Finally, Imogene admitted, "Probably not. I would have tried to find some other way to help him, but I probably wouldn't have kissed him." She realized she had just revealed to the old witch how entirely less-than-a-perfect-princess she was. "Does that mean you won't turn me back to my real form?"

The witch shrugged. "Makes no difference to me. I was just curious. I myself think it would be incredibly foolish for someone to sacrifice her life as a human for a boy she hardly knew."

With a sigh of relief that the question hadn't been a good-princess test, Imogene said, "So, you'll turn me back? Thank you! I'll tell my father what you said about the boys, and maybe he can assign a guard, or have a wall built, or decree it illegal for anyone to bother you, or . . ." Imogene's voice petered off when she saw that the witch was shaking her head.

"I wish I could help you," the witch said. "But when those four apples he threw hit me on the head like that, one after the other—*bonk! bonk! bonk! bonk!*—I lost my temper."

"Yes." Imogene nodded, but her little frog stomach was doing flip-flops. "So you said."

"I . . ." the old witch started. "Well, the fact is I cast the very first frogging spell that came to mind. Before really thinking things out. I can't just take it back. There is no charm to make it go away. I am so sorry. The only way for you to return to your own self is if someone kisses you and becomes a frog in your place. There is nothing I can do to change that."

Imogene sat down heavily. Well, as heavily as a frog can. Which isn't very.

Which was a good thing, because the witch was still holding her in her open palm.

"So there's nothing I can do?" Imogene asked. "I'm trapped?"

As though talking to someone of very limited intelligence, the witch spoke slowly and distinctly. She said, "You can get someone else to kiss you."

Then she said, "That way, that person will be a frog in your place."

And then she said, "At which point, you yourself will no longer be a frog."

"I understand," Imogene said. "But I couldn't do that to someone."

The witch considered this, then asked, "Because of the

whole twelve-going-on-thirteen-so-you're-not-big-into-kissing thing?"

"No," Imogene said. "Because it's wrong."

Once again the witch enunciated very carefully. "Nooo. That *is* the correct way to break this particular spell."

"I don't mean *wrong* wrong," Imogene explained. "I mean . . . you know . . . wrong."

"Ah! Now that you've clarified that . . ." the witch said.

But after a few moments, she added, "If it was me, I would give serious consideration to how to turn this back on the boy who started all this — the wainwright's boy."

That's only fair, Imogene thought. Sort of. She supposed. Or at least it was one way of looking at things.

"Maybe," she agreed. "But even so, I think that under the circumstances, he won't be very inclined to go about kissing any frogs, even if I managed to hide my identity."

"Good point," the witch admitted. She thought some more, then suggested, "Perhaps you could take turns with someone. I'm guessing the wainwright's boy probably wouldn't work out for this, which is a pity. But maybe other friends, or family members, might be willing to share the enchantment. For example, you could be a frog on Mondays, Wednesdays, and Fridays. Your father could substitute for you on Tuesdays, your mother on Thursdays, and your little brother on the weekends. Maybe this Prince Malcolm might want to give being a frog a try the next time his family comes to visit. It could be a learning and bonding experience for all of you."

"I don't think so," Imogene said.

"Sure, shoot down all my ideas," the witch said. She shrugged. "But, really, that's neither here nor there. You'll choose as you choose, and, after all, it's nothing to do with me."

Imogene nearly choked on a "Rrr-bitt," so angry she could spit. Except she didn't know if frogs *could* spit. She suspected her tongue might get in the way. Just to be safe, she limited herself to spitting out words. "*Nothing to do with you? It's your* spell."

"But it's *your* problem, dear." The witch leaned over to set Imogene into the grass. "You're welcome to stay in my well, if you'd like. I'll try to remember to leave the bucket halfway up, so you can come and go as you please. If you decide to go elsewhere, I'd suggest you stick to backyards.

Not so straightforward as the road, but the pond is off in that direction. That means the ground is just generally wetter, and you're not so likely to dry out. But, of course, that's your choice, too. Now shoo! Go away! I've got my own life to live."

"Well, so do I!" Imogene protested, hating the way that came out whiny, but still . . .

And yet the witch once again missed the point entirely. "Well, good," she said cheerily. "I'm so glad that's settled." She picked up her book and once more began reading, apparently able to forget Imogene the instant she wasn't looking at her.

"All right," Imogene said, "be that way." Which was a pointless thing to say. Obviously the witch *was* going to be that way.

Imogene hopped to the well, then up onto the edge, then into the bucket. Not that she was going to stay here. Even if she was to spend the rest of her life as a frog, she would not spend it with the witch as her companion, as that would be entirely exasperating. She splashed about in the water, getting her skin thoroughly wet, and drinking until she felt ready to burst, even though one part of her human mind taunted her that she'd just been squishing that same water with her webbed toes: *You're drinking your bath water!*

When she was satisfied that she was as moistened inside and out as was froggily possible, she jumped back down to the ground. She even ate a fly or two.

She considered ignoring the witch's advice and heading for the road, since that was more the direction she needed to go. But she'd already sampled its dangers. She shouldn't ignore good advice just because she didn't like who it came from.

"Goodbye!" Imogene croaked to the witch. "And thanks for all your help!"

Without taking her gaze off the page, the witch raised her hand in a halfhearted wave, not even giving Imogene the satisfaction of recognizing her sarcasm.

Chapter 5

A Princess Knows How to Engage in Interesting Conversation

(Not everybody has something interesting to say)

Imogene jumped her way to the back of the witch's yard, which was a bit soggy. *These webbed feet are quite handy,* she thought. And then wondered if feet *could* be handy.

A few hundred jumps and three gnats and a fly farther on, she reached the stream that would widen into a pond when it got near the mill.

Well, she reminded herself, *I AM a frog.*

That part was obvious.

I am a frog who knows how to swim.

That took a little more reminding.

At first she swam very near the edge of the stream, where

the water was shallow. But her toes kept getting tangled in the grass that grew there precisely because it was so shallow.

After a while, where the stream grew wider, she noticed there were other frogs.

"Hello," she called, because she didn't think she should be snobbish just because they had been born frogs and she had been born a princess.

The frogs didn't answer.

Then she realized they *were* talking, but in frog, not human. Fortunately, though the spell that the witch had cast let her continue to speak as a human, it also let her understand a few words of frog. By concentrating, she could make out what the frogs were saying, and that was when she realized their language only *had* a few words. Imogene didn't like to judge, but she felt that the frogs didn't have much to say.

The thing she heard most often was "Good food!" But she quickly recognized there were no frog words to make a distinction between *bug* or *worm,* or—even more important, she thought—between *Found some!* and *Looking for some!* Occasionally she would hear "Ouch!" when someone landed badly, and there was one group of male frogs chorusing over and over a croak that Imogene could only interpret as "Hey, girls! Big, strong males here! Good for producing likely-to-survive offspring!" The female frogs didn't answer: those who were interested swam over, and those who were not didn't.

There was no way for communicating such things as *Hello*, or *My, what a pretty shade of green you are*, or *Please excuse any unintentional rude behavior—I'm new to being a frog.*

All of a sudden, several of the frogs croaked, "Sky!" Or, Imogene wondered, would simply *Up!* be a more accurate translation? The frogs didn't seem to have much of a grasp of the world.

It was only when a shadow passed over her that she took into account the higher pitch of their croaks, a tone that she knew—once she thought about it—signified *Danger!*

Some of the frogs had dived below the surface of the water. Others remained perfectly still, pretending to be a bit of dead debris afloat in the stream, boring and unappetizing.

There was no time for her to seek the safety of going underwater, which she judged the more likely defense: any movement now would be sure to attract the predator. Which also meant that Imogene had to fight the inclination to raise her head to track what had to be a bird swooping in for lunch. Whether it was a hawk or a seagull or any other type of bird who ate frogs, what difference would knowing make? But it was hard *not* to know.

If it's coming after me, it's coming after me, Imogene reasoned, then she simultaneously braced herself to die and sent out and upward to the incoming bird the mental thought, *The male frogs are fatter!*

The shadow passed entirely over her—but barely. It was a heron, which explained why its shadow was so long, and it hit the water no farther away than the breadth of one of Imogene's hands—one of her human hands, true, but that was still terrifyingly close—and it snatched up one of the frogs who had hidden underwater. "Ouch!" was the only thing the frog said.

Imogene felt a little bit sad that someone had gotten eaten, but a whole lot glad that it hadn't been her.

As soon as the heron and its meal were airborne, the frogs in the stream resumed what they'd been doing. "Good food!" and "Hey, girls!" once more rang out over the water. Not a single *Poor Fred* or even an *Oh my!*

Imogene, however, was shaken. She paddled her froggy

legs to the edge of the water. There could well be snakes and other dangers on the land, she realized. And no frogs to croak out a warning. But she felt less exposed on the marshy ground than in the open water.

She could even see the back of a house from here. And a boy, throwing meal out to some chickens.

Imogene had had enough of trying to solve her problems on her own. She would go to this boy and ask him to transport her back to the castle. Surely her parents or one of her parents' various advisors would be able to come up with some solution.

And, she told herself as she began to jump toward him, a boy who lived so close to the house of the witch must certainly be used to seeing unusual things. He would not be as likely as other villagers to take alarm at a talking frog who claimed to be the princess of the realm.

She jumped through the marsh grass, then through the tall grass that bordered the marsh, then through the grass that formed the yard—cropped shorter by the goat that almost stepped on her because Imogene was concentrating on the boy so much that she didn't see the goat till the last moment.

Oh, don't go inside, Imogene mentally begged the boy, because she could see that he'd finished feeding the chickens.

Fortunately, the boy was not a conscientious worker: he hoisted himself onto the top rail of the fence that kept the goat away from his mother's wash line, and sat watching the chickens. Since chickens are not all that interesting, this had to be pure laziness on the boy's part, but it worked out to Imogene's advantage.

"Hello," she called to the boy.

He made a startled little jump and gave what Imogene could tell was a guilty-for-sitting-down-on-the-job glance around the yard. Then he hurriedly upended the meal bucket and shook it as though the only reason he'd sat was to give himself the chance to get every last bit of meal out for the chickens.

"Hello," Imogene repeated.

The boy looked from the back of the house to the yard, no doubt trying to determine where the voice was coming from, since no one was in sight.

By then Imogene had reached the fence. "Over here," she said. "By the gate. Look down." She figured that directly by the fence post was a safe place where the boy was unlikely to accidentally step on her. And if somehow he looked likely to, she could hop backwards beneath the lowest rail into the other section of the yard.

But the boy didn't get to his feet at all. "Oh," he said. "What do *you* want?"

Well! Imogene thought. There was not being frightened because one was used to seeing unusual things from living next door to a witch, and there was sounding downright bored—at a talking frog.

She fell back onto her previous statement. "Hello," she said once more, this time speaking in her most formal princess voice.

The boy gave a soft grunt, which could have been a return greeting, or a sound of mild indigestion.

Imogene decided to take the sound, whatever it was, as encouragement. "I'm relieved to see that you're not troubled at my appearance, because I've had a rather unfortunate experience with a witch, and—"

The boy interrupted, "Go on, Harry. What're you playing at?"

Harry? The only Harry she knew was the wainwright's boy. "Oh," said Imogene. Then, remembering how Harry had described the witch as living just down the road from his friend, she said, "Oh, you must be Tolf."

The boy rolled his eyes. "Same as I been all my life."

"Hello, Tolf. I know this might be hard to believe, though not so hard as it might be for someone who lives elsewhere, but I'm Princess Imogene."

Tolf snorted. "Yeah, and I'm King Wellington."

Startled, Imogene took time to consider. Since her world had been turned upside down, it was, in theory, possible that her father . . .

But, no, it wasn't. Tolf talked like a peasant, not a king; and Tolf wasn't overjoyed to see his daughter safe—if somewhat froggified—which her father would have been.

Tolf, she realized, was mocking her.

"No, really," she said.

"Yeah?" Tolf said, in a tone he no doubt thought was really clever. "Then how'd you know my name? Explain that, why doncha? How would a princess know *my* name?"

"Harry told me."

"Oooh," Tolf said. "'Harry told me.' Pretty convenient, that, since you *are* Harry. But I gotta say, Harry, you almost got that posh princess voice down pat. A little bit overdone to be absolutely believable, but good."

Imogene had had just about enough of this nonsense. "Look—" she started.

But Tolf interrupted. "No, you look, Harry. I already told you: I'm not calling my sister out here and telling her, 'Hey, Luella, I bet you're too scared to kiss this here frog.' 'Cause once she did, then Luella would turn around and find some unsuspecting fella to kiss *her*—and, believe me, Luella's pretty good at finding fellas to kiss her, and I don't think a little setback like being a frog would slow her down much. Once she was a girl again, she'd tell Ma how I tricked her, and—whew!—would Ma tan my hide!"

"I am *not* Harry. I am Princess Imogene Eustacia Wellington."

"Yeah, well, *I* ain't kissing you, neither, Harry, even if you're pretending to be a girl. You got yourself into this mess. You get yourself out."

"I'm not asking you to kiss me!" Imogene shouted in her loudest croak. "All I'm asking is for you to take me home, back to the castle, so my parents—"

"Yeah, yeah," Tolf said. "Give it up, Harry. You'll never convince the king and queen, neither. And if you did, once they found you out, you'd be in even worse trouble than you are now. You haven't thought this out. Soon's you get someone in the castle to kiss you and you turn into Harry the wainwright's boy instead of Her High and Mighty Highness Princess Imogene Etc., Etc.—whew! That'd be even worse than my Ma finding out I'd tricked Luella into becoming a frog."

"But—"

"Gotta go, Harry." Tolf jumped off the fence rail and headed back toward the house.

"But—"

"Good luck to ya."

"But—"

The door slammed shut behind him.

"You're dumb as a post, Tolf," Imogene muttered. For good measure, she added, "I'd be willing to stay a frog for ninety-nine years rather than kiss you!"

But then she thought about what she'd just said. And she wondered if staying a frog was exactly what was going to happen to her.

Chapter 6

A Princess Must Be Assertive and Persuasive, Though Never Pushy

(Yeah, lots of luck with that one)

*B*oys! Imogene thought. *They're all just about entirely useless.*

She wondered if she'd have any better luck with Tolf's sister, Luella. Or with his parents. But there was no telling if any of them were even home, much less if they would prove any easier to convince than Tolf.

Still, she thought, *what do I have to lose?* The sun was quite low in the sky, and back home at the castle servants would no doubt be in a frenzy of getting-supper-ready-to-serve-to-the-royal-family activity. Her absence would be noticed soon, if it hadn't been already. She needed to avoid having her parents worrying about her. Because she had come to learn that parents can act strangely: if they're worried that something bad has happened to their child but it turns out that this is not the case, parents permit themselves one brief moment of relief, followed by hours of *How could yous* and reprimands and "consequences"—which is a fancy word for "punishments." If Imogene was to avoid this, she had no time to lose.

She jumped closer to the house and examined the door through which Tolf had entered. Unfortunately, he had closed it tight behind him. Where was the boy's carelessness when she could use it? She positioned herself directly below the window at the back of the house. "Hello!" she called. "Announcing a royal reward for doing a small service for Princess Imogene." Her frog voice did not carry so much as her human voice did—which her mother habitually complained she could hear throughout the castle—and no one came to investigate.

So Imogene jumped her way around to the front. But the front door was closed, too.

Even the door to the small barn in the side yard—home, no doubt, to the chickens and the goat—was shut.

And, now that she thought about it, that was unusual. Most people only closed the barn door at night and in harsh weather, leaving it open during the day just in case the animals wanted to get out of the sun or rain.

Even odder: though the door was closed, the latch was not secured.

Maybe someone was in there, she thought, perhaps a member of Tolf's family preparing the barn for housing the animals overnight. Still, without windows and with the door shut, anyone in there would be working in the dark.

Imogene hopped closer. "Hello!" she called from directly outside the door.

Someone *was* in there, she was sure of it, because she heard faint stirrings. Not faint as in mice running for cover, but faint as in humans trying to be quiet.

"Hello," Imogene repeated. "Anyone here?"

From inside the barn, a male voice answered, "No."

Someone shushed him.

Imogene used the only name she had. "Luella?"

The same male voice whispered frantically to whoever was in the barn with him, "It's your mother."

A female voice, presumably Tolf's sister, Luella, hissed back, "It's not."

"Well, it's somebody looking for you." The voice made the speaker sound well-spoken, if not exactly bright.

Some more shushing, this time more insistent.

Imogene said, "I can hear you."

After sighing loudly enough that Imogene could hear that, too, the girl Luella called out, "Everything's fine in here. Um, no need to come in. I'm just doing a little bit of . . . oh . . . fluffing up the straw for the goat here. Alone." A forced laugh. "Of course. Of course, I'm alone. Why wouldn't I be? All by myself. I'll be finished in a bit. So, um, why don't you wait for me in front of the house?"

Well, obviously something was going on that shouldn't have been.

Imogene would have declared it none of her business and gone elsewhere—except she had nowhere else to go. Back to the pond, with the frogs and the frog-eating birds? Back on the road, where there were cats and dogs and wagons and people flinging radishes? Back to the witch, who was no help at all—and annoying as well? Imogene told the people in the barn, "Oh, all right. I'll leave and go wait patiently by the house."

"*In front of* the house," Luella reminded, since that faced the other direction and someone standing there would not be able to see the barn door.

"In front," Imogene agreed.

After a brief pause, she heard the male voice whisper, "Is she gone? I didn't hear her leave."

Of course they hadn't heard her leave. There was nothing Imogene could do about that. Frog footsteps—even annoyed frog footsteps, even annoyed-teenage-girl-frogs-stamping-their-feet footsteps are generally quieter than the most attentively-trying-to-be-secret human footsteps.

"She must be gone," the male voice stated, maybe in reaction to a headshake or a shrug from Luella. "Inquire whether she's still there."

Luella tried to hush her friend. "Bertie!" she complained.

Imogene tapped her little webbed foot impatiently.

Eventually Luella and this Bertie must have agreed that if they waited much longer, the person who had been out there would come back. Imogene heard someone—someone with big galumphing boots—tiptoe to the door. She stood her ground, but attentively, ready to jump off to the side if those boots started heading toward her.

The door was pushed open a crack. Imogene caught a glimpse of blond hair as a young man poked his head out, then in, so fast he couldn't have seen anything and might in fact have only succeeded in making himself dizzy. He repeated the movement, marginally slower. Then once again, this time sweeping his gaze over the yard.

"Gone," he announced to Luella, still hidden somewhere behind him inside the barn, "whoever she was."

He pushed the door the rest of the way open, and Imogene caught her first good look at them.

They were both older than she was, maybe even sixteen or seventeen years old—just about adults—which meant that the young man, Bertie, was not nearly as old as Imogene had guessed from his voice, which was deep and rich and more refined than Luella's. Imogene realized she'd been picturing someone like Sir Denley, who proclaimed the news in the town square and announced visitors to the castle on state occasions. Luella was pretty in a clean-faced, bosomy sort of way that reminded Imogene of Tolf's comment that his sister would not have trouble finding someone to kiss her. And as for Bertie . . . Imogene suspected the young man never had trouble in that area, either. His clothes were fancier than most farmers wore—especially the hat, which sported an ostrich plume.

"Hello," Imogene said.

Luella squealed. Bertie took a step back into the barn.

"Please don't be frightened," Imogene told them. As soon as the words were out of her mouth, she could have kicked herself for saying them. Except, of course, that frogs aren't built in a way that she *could* have kicked herself. The trouble was, she knew that many adults—and, she suspected many almost-adults—didn't like to admit to being frightened. She started over again. "I'm sorry to have startled you—"

But Luella, peering over the arm Bertie had extended in readiness to slam the barn door shut, asked in a tone somewhere between fear and distaste, "What's *that?*"

"It's a frog," Bertie said, after glancing around the yard to make sure that's all it was.

"Frogs don't talk," Luella said.

"Well, you see—" Imogene started.

Luella continued right over her, saying to Bertie, "I ain't never heard of a frog that could talk. Have you?"

Apparently Bertie was the sort who could never bring himself to say "I don't know," who always had to be an expert about everything and always had to have the last word. "Well, yes," he said in his authoritative voice. "As a matter of fact, I have."

Imogene and Luella both looked at him skeptically.

Bertie continued, as though amazed that Luella didn't know what he was talking about. "African speaking frogs?" he said.

Luella shook her head.

For that matter, so did Imogene.

Bertie said, "I would have thought news of such a marvel would have spread by now, even to a backward place like this. You see, the troupe of actors to which I belong often performs in front of emperors and kings and dukes. Such people go mad over anything new. The latest fashion is to have a parrot, which is a colorful bird from the deepest jungles of Africa. And parrots can be trained to talk. Not intelligently, like people, but they can repeat what they've heard."

Imogene thought, *Yes, well, not all people can speak intelligently.*

And sure enough, Luella, squinting at Imogene, spoke up. "I heard of parrots, Bertie. This is not *that* backwards of a place. But this is a frog, Bertie, not a bird."

Bertie proved he was not the sort to ever back down from a debate. "I'm getting to that, my sweet. So in high society there's always one duchess who wants to out-fashion another, and the very newest thing is to have a speaking frog from remotest China."

"I thought you said it was an *African* speaking frog."

"No, the parrots are from Africa; the frogs are from China."

"You said Africa."

Bertie considered. "Yes, my treasure, but the Chinese part of Africa."

Imogene cut into the bickering. "Excuse me for interrupting," she said, "but actually I'm from right here. You see, I'm Princess Imogene, and—"

Luella asked Bertie, "If it's a Chinese speaking frog, then how come I can understand what it's saying? How come it don't speak Chinese?"

"My love," Bertie told her, "it's like a parrot. It doesn't know what it's saying. It's only repeating sounds. Just as not all parrots speak African. It all depends on how they've been trained—and by whom."

"I don't know . . ." Luella said, unconvinced.

"Excuse me," Imogene repeated. "I am not African or Chinese. I come from just around the corner, the castle up on that little hill. You can see the one turret from here. I've had a spell put on me . . ." This time she interrupted herself when Bertie stooped down to take her in his hand.

Hmm, Imogene thought, wondering if it was a good idea to let him do that. But she was also thinking that—face to face—it might be easier to convince him of who she was, and what she was not.

"See," Bertie said, holding Imogene out on his palm to Luella, who shrank back as though Imogene had sharp teeth and claws, "notice the smooth skin. Frogs from around here have warts. Chinese frogs don't."

Imogene corrected him, "*Most* frogs don't. *Toads* have warts. But I'm not either a frog or a toad. I'm a princess. *Your* princess. Princess Imogene Eu—"

"Isn't she adorable?" Bertie asked.

Which is a nice thing to have someone say about you, whether you're a frog or a princess or someone in between.

"I suppose," Luella said.

Before Imogene could tell them, *That's very kind of you,* Bertie got a quizzical look on his face and said, "Or he."

Which was not nearly so nice a thing to have someone say, no matter what kind of girl you are.

Bertie picked Imogene up with his other hand and held her upside down, and that was downright humiliating as well as dizzying. He said, "Hard to tell with a Chinese speaking frog. But I suppose we might as well call it 'she' since it sounds like a girl."

Still upside down, Imogene told both of them, "I am most definitely a girl. I am Princess Imogene Eustacia—"

Somehow or other Bertie had talked himself into believing his own story. He interrupted once more. "She will be a sensation at our performances. Now all we need is a bucket . . ."

"Performances?" Imogene said. "Bucket?"

"See?" Bertie told Luella, finally righting Imogene. "She's learning new words, which she will now be able to repeat, just as I told you." Then, as Luella handed him a bucket, he said, "Perfect!" and dropped Imogene in. "And the headscarf from your pack, please."

It must have been the bucket from which the animals were expected to drink, for there was water in it. Imogene, who had not expected any of this, sputtered a bit as she came up to the surface, and she tried reason one more time, saying, "I'm sure my parents will pay you generously—"

And taking the time to say that cost her the last chance to escape, for Bertie tied Luella's scarf over the opening of the bucket, so that Imogene could breathe, could hear, could even see a tiny bit of daylight through the weave of the fabric. But she could not hop out.

Bertie said, "Now let us go, my love, before your parents return and try to stop us from embarking on our grand adventure."

Even though he'd said *my love*, it took Imogene a moment to realize he was talking to Luella, and not her, since Imogene's parents would *certainly* try to stop Bertie from taking their daughter away in a bucket.

He asked, "Can you manage your pack while I carry the bucket?"

Apparently Luella could. "This is so exciting!" she said.

"Running away from home with you to join your company of actors! I can't believe that someone the likes of me will have a chance to see the world, like you talked about! To perform in front of all them emperors and such! Won't my family turn green with envy?"

Imogene didn't bother saying that Luella and her parents didn't know the first thing about turning green. "See the world?" she screamed up through the scarf as Luella closed the barn door and started walking. "You can't take me away from my home and my family!"

"I see what you mean, Bertie," Luella cooed, lacing her arm around Bertie's, so that the bucket with Imogene in it jostled with every step the two of them took. "She is a most clever little Chinese froggy." Despite acknowledging Imogene as a frog, Luella said in a parroty voice, "See the world! *Awk!* See the world!" Then she told Bertie, "With your experience on the stage, and what you'll teach me about being an actor, and with this frog—we are going to make us a fortune! And we don't *never* have to come back home!"

Chapter 7

A Princess Should Always Be Open to New Experiences

(There are experiences, and then there are experiences)

Eventually Imogene wearied of shouting. The scarf Bertie and Luella had tied over the bucket's opening to keep her from jumping out made her prison a bit dark and stuffy. They'd put a rock in there so that she could climb up out of the water, but they had a terrible tendency to jostle and tip the bucket as they walked so that she kept slipping off the rock, and—once she was in the water—she became a floating target who had to dodge the rock as it bounced around the confined space. Besides, nothing she said could convince them that she was Princess Imogene Eustacia Wellington, and her throat was beginning to get scratchy. Frog throats are not meant to carry on in human language, and she saw exactly what Harry had meant when he'd complained early in their acquaintance that shouting to get her attention had given him that ticklish need-to-clear-your-throat sensation that people refer to as having a frog in the throat.

From the depths of her bucket and through her scarf, Imogene heard Luella ask, "Are we almost there yet, Bertie?"

"Almost, my dear," Bertie assured her.

"It's just your friends seem to have chosen such an out-of-the-way spot to camp in. I'd have thought they'd stay in town. In the castle, even. Like you said they usually do when they put on a play for kings and queens."

Imogene suspected that Bertie's acting troupe was not quite so famous and respected as he had been indicating. She spoke up, saying, "No actors have performed or are due to perform at the castle." But even as she said it, she knew Luella wouldn't believe her about that, either.

And, sure enough, Luella ignored her comment and moved on to a different topic. "What should we name her, Bertie?" Luella asked.

Once more Imogene couldn't keep silent. "Imogene," she croaked at them.

"She does seem rather stuck on that," Bertie observed.

Luella said, "Which *I* think is cute, and *you* think is cute, but what if the royal family finds that offensive?" She thought for a moment. "Ooo, I know! How about Polly, like she was a parrot?" Then, in the kind of voice quite a few people use for pets and very young children, Luella said, "Can you say 'Polly'? Say: 'My name is Polly.'"

Imogene couldn't help herself. "You," she told Luella, "are a twit."

But Luella only laughed.

"Better be careful," Bertie said. "Some parrots have picked up quite rude language. The same might be true for our Chinese speaking frog."

Imogene told him, "You're a twit, too."

Bertie said, "Since she's already trained to say her name is Princess Imogene, why don't we just go with that? We'll be on to the next kingdom soon, anyway."

Imogene groaned and clung on to her constantly shifting rock.

Till finally, after the light had grown so dim Imogene feared the sun had set, and after two more *Are we there yets?* from Luella, they found where Bertie's friends had camped.

"Oh," Luella said, and Imogene could tell from her tone that she was surprised in a not-a-good-surprise way. "It doesn't look nearly so grand as I imagined."

"Well, it's night," Bertie pointed out.

"Yes, but you kept talking about the wagon, and this is just a cart, like my father uses to haul pigs and produce to market."

"Surely you didn't think you were going to ride in it?" Bertie said in a tone that indicated if Luella *had* been thinking that, then she was more foolish than she ought to admit to. "This is to carry the costumes and props for the plays. We people of the theater always walk, which gives us the chance to rehearse our lines as we travel."

"I see," Luella said. But she still sounded disappointed.

"Here," Bertie said, "let me introduce you to Ned, the leader of our troupe."

Luella stopped walking so abruptly that the bucket with

Imogene in it slapped against either Luella's or Bertie's leg. Water and rock and Imogene all sloshed dizzyingly. "But, Bertie, I thought you said *you* was the head of the troupe."

"No, my precious. I'm the lead actor. Ned . . . is more an administrator, or manager." They resumed walking, and Bertie called out, "Ned!"

A new voice greeted them—not warmly. "Well, Bert, you took your time getting here. You said you were going to be back early enough to help strike the set and pack from the last town and to take your turn pushing the wagon. I almost thought you'd given up on the performing life and that you'd decided to settle in as a farmer."

Bertie ignored the complaints. "Ned, this is Luella, of whom I spoke. Luella . . . Ned."

From the way the bucket bobbed, Luella must have curtsied. "Pleased, I'm sure," she cooed.

Ned grunted.

Bertie explained, "Luella's parents took longer than we thought to leave to go visit the aged aunt. And then her brother took forever to feed the chickens while we were required to take refuge in the barn."

Ned growled, "Bert, you *always* make a production of *everything*."

The bucket was being jostled as Luella nudged Bertie. "Show 'im what we got, Bertie. Show 'im."

"Ah! Take a look at this, Ned." Bertie peeled the scarf partway off the bucket—partway, so that Imogene didn't have room to jump out and away.

Which she wouldn't have. She was too startled by seeing that the sky was black, with a sprinkling of stars. She'd supposed that the scarf had been filtering out most of the light, but the sun had set—it was totally night. By now, she knew, her parents would have gone from being annoyed at her lateness to genuine worry.

"Ta-dah!" Luella said.

Imogene saw a man probably a little bit younger than her father peer into the bucket at her. He stroked his beard and said, "I can't really make out . . ."

"It's a Chinese speaking frog!" Luella announced.

"A what?"

"A Chinese speaking frog!"

The face withdrew. "What are you going on about?" Ned asked Luella.

"Listen to this," Luella told him. Then to Imogene she said, in that same annoying singsong she'd come to use with her, "What's your name?"

Well, Imogene thought, *if they don't believe I'm a princess frog, and if they think a Chinese speaking frog is worth keeping in order to show, let's see what they think of a regular frog.* She said, "Rrr-bitt."

"No," Luella corrected her gently, then prompted her, "Princess . . . ? Your name is Princess . . . ?"

Imogene just looked at her.

Obviously hoping she could outsmart a frog, Luella said, "Is your name Polly? Does Polly want a cracker?"

A mosquito came in close to investigate, and Imogene shot her tongue out and ate it.

Ned sighed. Loudly. He told Bertie, "Fine woman you've found for yourself there, Bert. A most suitable match for you." He shook his head and walked away.

"Maybe she's tired," Luella said.

"Perhaps," Bertie agreed.

Luella told Imogene, "Nighty-night. Nighty-night, Princess Imogene." She refastened the scarf, destroying Imogene's hope that during the night, unobserved, she might have been able to work her way out the opening Bertie had uncovered.

Drat! Imogene thought.

She spent the next few hours jumping against the scarf, trying to dislodge it, until finally, exhausted, she fell asleep on her rock. The only good thing—the absolutely *only* good thing—was that it was just in Imogene's dreams that the rock grew legs and chased her around the bucket.

The next morning, when Luella once more pulled back a corner of the scarf, Imogene fought back the only way she could, by promptly greeting her with another, "Rrrr-bittt!"

"Bertie!" Luella complained. "She won't talk."

"Maybe she's hungry," Bertie suggested.

"What do frogs eat?"

"I don't know. Flies, I imagine. Bugs and beetles and so forth."

"Ooo," Luella said. "I think I saw a fly in the corner of the cart." She left Imogene in Bertie's safekeeping but promptly came back and tossed a crusty dead fly into the bucket.

Despite the fact that Imogene was very hungry, this fly looked even more unappetizing to her than the others she had eaten so far. Still, she forced her tongue out of her mouth, and she picked up the fly. She closed her mouth. She tried to swallow. She gagged, and the fly shot out of her mouth.

One of the other actors—Imogene saw there were three men, besides Bertie and Ned—had stopped to watch. He said, "I think they only eat live bugs."

Oh, Imogene thought. She hadn't realized that, but her frog body had.

"Oh," Luella said. Wearing a sad expression, she covered the bucket.

The man said, "I hope you feed *us* better than that."

"What?" Luella asked.

"Breakfast," the man said. "What tasty treat were you planning on preparing for us to give us the strength and stamina we need for a day on the road?"

"I wasn't planning on preparing you anything," Luella snapped.

"Aw, come on, please," the man wheedled. "You're the

only woman here, and the men, if I do say so myself, we're all terrible cooks."

"I suppose," Luella grumbled. "This once. But I didn't join up to cook for you. I'm going to be an actor."

The man barked out a laugh, but Bertie stepped in before the man could say any more. Bertie said, "Come, my love, let us do this together. We shall be a cooking ensemble. A duet of dining."

Hmm, Imogene thought. She'd seen several groups of professional actors, and they were always men. *All* men. If the play called for a woman, that part was played by a young man dressed like a woman. Some of them were very convincing. But Imogene, as princess, always got a front row seat, whether in the castle or in the town square, so she could see their Adam's apples and sometimes their beard stubble. Had Bertie failed to explain to Luella that women simply did not appear on the stage?

Throughout the day, Luella would open the bucket to throw in a leaf with an ant on it, or a ladybug, or a caterpillar. It was enough to sustain Imogene. Just barely.

In the evening, the group stopped at a small village. By

the sounds, Imogene could tell that they performed some acrobatics, juggling, and magic tricks.

Luella had removed the scarf from the bucket so that she could reach in and stroke Imogene's head, when Bertie returned. "No play?" the farm girl who wanted to act asked, with a bit of whine in her tone. "No acting?"

"Too small a venue," Bertie said. "Any who have trod the boards know to save our creative energies for the bigger towns." Then, though his meaning had been perfectly clear, he explained. "*Trod the boards* is the way we theater folk refer to putting on a play." He flashed a smile and said, "Can you sew this button back on for me, my darling?"

Luella hesitated, but took the shirt Bertie was holding out to her.

"And, while you're at it, shorten the sleeves?"

Imogene, doing the back float in the bucket, saw Luella narrow her eyes at Bertie, who either didn't notice or pretended not to. He asked, "How's the frog doing?"

Imogene spoke up for herself. "Rrr-bitt!" she said.

"Well," Bertie told Luella, "if it's lost the ability to speak, I suppose all it's good for now is to eat."

Imogene was so horrified, for a moment she lost the ability to speak in human or frog.

Luella, fortunately, was also horrified, but not to the point of speechlessness. "Bertie! No!"

"I'm just saying," Bertie murmured.

They argued a bit about that, and about whether Luella should make supper for the group once she finished mending Bertie's shirt. In the end, Luella won one argument and lost the other: she made supper, but it didn't involve Chinese speaking frog.

When Luella lifted the scarf the following morning, Imogene was ready. She jumped—right out of the bucket and onto the ground, prepared to start jumping toward home. But then she hesitated. Nothing looked at all familiar.

Had they traveled east or west? Was that a river they were camped beside?

Imogene circled, trying to get her bearings.

Luella dropped the scarf over her, trapping her in the folds of fabric.

Bertie called, "Luella, my turtledove, don't let it get

away. I am so tired of warm mutton stew for supper and cold mutton stew for breakfast, I would give anything in exchange for a savory dish of leeks and crisp frog legs."

"No," Luella said, scooping up scarf and frog. "You can't eat something what knows its own name."

"But it doesn't," Bertie pointed out. "Not anymore it doesn't. Maybe they forget how to talk once they reach a certain age."

Imogene couldn't stop trembling, unsure what to do.

"I think she's homesick," Luella argued. She shook the scarf out over the bucket so that Imogene fell back in. "I think this isn't what she expected, and she's missing home."

Bertie folded his arms across his chest. "It will get better, oh apple of my eye. We'll be at a big town the day after tomorrow. And then we'll put on"—he held his arms out expansively—"a play!"

"And will I have a part in it?"

"Oh, yes," Bertie said without hesitation.

"All right," Luella said. "But you ain't eating the frog."

"But, my love bunny, it's such a burden for you to carry that bucket, to be looking for flies and such all the time. The others are beginning to talk. And look, the poor thing has begun to get pale and pasty. Better to eat it now than to watch it waste away."

He had a point, Imogene knew. Not about eating her, of course, but that she was slowly fading from lack of proper nourishment, and from being cooped up in a small bucket with the same old water she'd been in for two days now. Not to mention that slippery, bouncing rock.

Luella hugged the bucket to her chest and spoke to Imogene in a voice little more than a whisper. "Please get better, little froggy. Please eat, and be happy, and speak. I could keep you in something bigger than this bucket, and let you run loose once in a while so's you could chase after your own food—food that's more to your liking—if I wasn't a-feared you'd run away."

Bertie tugged the bucket away from her. "Luella," he said, in the firm voice of a grownup wanting a child to be-have, to accept something he knew she wouldn't like.

The time for silence had passed. Imogene spoke up. "All right. All right, I'll talk." She sighed. "And I promise I won't try to run away."

And that was how Princess Imogene Eustacia Welling-ton joined a traveling band of performers.

Chapter 8

A Princess Is as Good as Her Word

(Which word would that be?)

Luella sent Bertie to fetch Ned and the other actors.

Imogene allowed herself to grow hopeful. Surely, she told herself, these actors were likely to have more sense than Luella and Bertie. Actually, she was fairly confident that just about *anyone* was likely to have more sense than Luella and Bertie. The actors would have traveled and seen the world, which she was almost certain wasn't the case with Bertie, no matter what he said; and they wouldn't be so set on making themselves look important. Surely people like that would be sophisticated enough not to believe in a Chinese speaking frog. She could convince them about what had happened to her. And they would return her to her home—and even if they wouldn't do so because it was the right thing to do, at least they would do it for the royal reward they would receive.

But she quickly saw she was not off to a good start. Apparently the men had discovered one of the wheels on the cart was wobbly, and they had been trying to fix it when Bertie interrupted them. Now they made no attempt to hide their impatience as they followed him back to where Luella sat on the ground holding Imogene in her hand, and Ned was striding briskly, demanding even before he got there, "This better be good, Bert."

Princess Imogene cleared her throat and said, "Hello, Ned. And you other actors. Bertie and Luella wanted me to talk for you."

Ned stopped so quickly, the other three men walked into him, one right after the other. Then he looked from Imogene to Bertie to Imogene and back to Bertie. "How did you do that?" he asked Bertie.

Luella laughed. "Bertie ain't doing nothing, Ned. It's the frog. Tell 'im your name, clever froggy."

Imogene said, "I'm Princess Imogene Eustacia Wellington. And, actually, I am *not* a clever froggy. I am a princess who has had a spell put on me by a witch."

Ned's look of amazement broadened into a grin. Speaking to Bertie, he asked, "How did you ever train a frog to croak in a way that sounds so much like words?"

While Imogene took the time to stamp a little green foot irritably, Bertie said, "Well, it required patience and persistence, but in the end I *am* quite pleased with the results."

Luella looked as surprised as Imogene felt at this version of the story; but Luella recovered first. "She's a Chinese speaking frog. She already knew a lot of words when we found her."

Bertie continued, "I mean, it made a few almost-human sounds, so I diligently kept coaching it."

Imogene's temper snapped. She shouted at Ned, at all of them, "There is no such thing as a Chinese speaking frog!"

Her mother would have told her, "A princess does not shout like a common fishwife."

Ned, however, was plainly pleased. "Well, well. This is fine, indeed. We'll try easing the little creature into our program tonight. It should be a sensation!" He picked up both scarf and bucket from where Luella had set them on the ground and said, "Let us put the frog back in here, then we can pack this in the cart so that there's no chance of the little fellow getting loose."

Little fellow?

No chance of getting loose?

Before Imogene had time to be offended or worried, Luella stood. But even though she stepped forward, that was for emphasis, not surrender, for she still held Imogene protectively. "I promised her a bigger bucket in return for her promise not to try to escape."

Ned roared with laughter. "The frog promised not to try to escape?"

"Yes," Luella said.

"Yes," Imogene said.

"Yes," even Bertie said.

"Dear Luella," Ned said, "what's a frog's word worth? I'd wager it isn't even as good as an actor's word."

Bertie looked as though he might be considering objecting, but he didn't.

Although she was beginning to suspect it was hopeless, Imogene told all of them, "But a princess is as good as her word!" As soon as she said it, she remembered it had been one of the chapter titles in *The Art of Being a Princess*. It seemed forever ago that her mother had presented her with the book in the hope that it would help her to get herself ready for her thirteenth birthday. Now here she was, two days closer to that birthday than she had been back then, remembering with some personal embarrassment how she had felt so bored by the book, so put-upon, so unfairly treated by life in general and by her mother in particular. What she wouldn't give to be back home, even if that meant being lectured on princessly behavior.

Luella was still arguing with Ned. "She's doing poorly in there. She needs more room."

Ned looked down at Imogene with an expression Imogene couldn't decipher.

Imogene told him, "Return me to my home, and my parents will reward you with a sum greater than you could earn in a year of play-acting."

And then she saw it: the flicker of understanding, of belief on Ned's face.

Finally! Imogene thought.

But when he spoke, it was to Luella, and what he said was, "If you clean out the big cooking pot, the cauldron, we can place the frog in there. It won't be able to climb out because of the way the sides curve in, but flies and whatnot can get in, and it can eat and be in the sunshine, since it shows a tendency not to talk when it's unhappy."

And yet he knew. Imogene saw it in his eyes. "But . . ." she sputtered, "but . . ."

Ned told his men, "We need to get that wheel fixed, or we won't be going anywhere. Bert, if you're not too busy doing whatever you habitually do to avoid being useful, perhaps you would deign to render us your aid? And, Luella, before you put the frog in the pot, you can make us breakfast."

"But . . ." Luella sputtered, sounding like an echo of Imogene, "but . . ."

Uh-huh, Imogene thought at her. *Good luck with that.*

&ventually, breakfast got made, the wheel got fixed, and the company got under way. That afternoon and the next, they were to visit small towns, whose names were unfamiliar to Imogene, so that was no help in letting her know where she was or how far from home. More worrisome was the fact that she did recognize the name of the bigger town they'd be in after that. Balton Keep was three kingdoms away. Still, her father knew King Salford of Balton Keep. If Imogene could hold on for the two days it would take to travel there, and if she could then get word to King Salford, he would see to it that she'd be returned home. It was the best chance she was likely to get.

Meanwhile, though Luella wouldn't believe Imogene's claim of being a princess, she *did* clearly believe Imogene's promise not to try to escape. So she let Imogene ride on her shoulder, much to Ned's displeasure, and that was far more interesting—even though this *was* Luella—than spending the whole day in a bucket or a pot.

Imogene said to her, "What do you know of the witch who lives just down the road from you?"

Luella shook her head. "I don't know that story."

"It's not a story," Imogene said. "There's a witch who lives just down the road from you."

"Really?" Luella said. "I didn't know that. The blacksmith lives just down the road. Have you seen him? The young one, I mean, not the father. He is *so* well built. Those arm and shoulder muscles, glistening with sweat and well-being . . ." Luella sighed and began to fan herself.

Imogene said, "The witch lives before the smithy. In the house with the apple trees in front."

"I haven't noticed an apple tree in anyone's yard," Luella admitted. "There's an oak tree where the cooper lives. I know that 'cause every autumn the cooper's nephew likes to throw acorns at me when I pass by. My friend Nell says that's a sure sign he likes me. Do you think so?" She didn't give Imogene a chance to answer. "I used to believe her when we were twelve, but now I'm sixteen, I'm not so sure. Even though he *is* cute, and I wouldn't mind him liking me. In the winter, there're always boys throwing snowballs at girls, and I don't think all those boys like all those girls. I mean, I suppose they *could* . . ."

Imogene tried to bring Luella back to the topic of the witch. "Between the cooper's house and the smithy," she clarified.

Luella's brow creased with concentration. "No," she finally said. "No, I don't think there're any cute boys that live in those houses . . ."

Well, that explained why Luella had not noticed any odd goings-on despite living so close to the witch. Apparently all she ever noticed were cute boys.

Which explained Bertie.

But Ned, Imogene thought. Ned knew there was no such thing as Chinese speaking frogs. Why was he pretending?

When they arrived at the village that afternoon, one of the actors took out a trumpet. He blew a fanfare or two in practice, and Bertie did some weird vocalizations (*"La-la-la-la-la. Me-me-me-me-me. Pie-pie-pie-pie-pie. Low-low-low-low-low. Lu-lu-lu-lu-lu."*) to prepare his voice, then the two of them walked together down the village street, announcing a performance.

Imogene was glad to see Bertie leave. He had refused most of the afternoon to speak to Luella, claiming he needed to focus, and this had made Luella cranky. Imogene wasn't sure what he was focusing on, but periodically he would strike a dramatic pose or he would suddenly declaim such things as "No! My loyalty to my king and my country means more to me than your filthy gold or your vile threats! You may go ahead and rip my body asunder—I shall not betray my liege lord!"

It was not a play with which Imogene was familiar, and she suspected it would not be much to her liking.

Villagers began to gather even before the heralds were back. Some pretended that they just happened to have come out on the village square by coincidence, but it was clear that this was more excitement than the people were used to.

Imogene had asked to be returned to her cauldron for one of her periodic dunkings, and she was swimming laps when Ned came and abruptly plucked her out of the water. It wasn't that he was rough, but he certainly wasn't as gentle as Luella, who generally announced herself by saying something like "Hello, little froggy. It's time to rejoin the *people* people," and then she would cup her hands in the water and raise them slowly, with the water draining out between her fingers until only Imogene remained. But Ned reached in one-handed without even announcing himself. And it was only when Imogene was dangling in the air that he said, "All right, my fine Chinese speaking frog, are you ready for your acting debut?"

While Imogene was a bit flustered, Luella's mood instantly improved. "Ooo," she said. "What do you have planned for us?"

"For *us*," Ned repeated flatly. Then he said, "Well, the

frog and I will sit out front and chat a bit for the entertainment of the villagers. Get them in a spending mood, if all goes well. And you will give this pot a good scrubbing, then see about supper for us once the performance is over."

"What?" Luella squealed. "No." She stamped her foot. "Froggy is my pet. "

Imogene didn't like being called a pet, even though she knew Luella didn't mean it badly.

Luella continued, "We found her in *my* parents' barn. I take care of her. Bertie said you'd help me make up an act with her. Like a small play. Her and me. Together. Not her and you. Bertie said."

Not sounding very impressed with this argument, Ned asked, "Did he, now?"

Imogene joined her voice to Luella's as they both said, "Yes, he did."

Ned laughed. "And so you shall," he agreed. "Someday. But for now I need to test the waters, so to speak. I daresay a frog—even a princess frog—can understand the necessity of testing the waters. See what's what. See what floats and what sinks like a stone."

Pouting, Luella pointed out, "You could do that by watching me."

"And so I could," Ned said. "Just. Not. Today."

Not today was the kind of thing Imogene's parents said when they didn't want to come right out and say *no*. Imogene wondered if Luella's *someday* for performing would come any sooner than her own *someday* for getting a pet monkey such as the one Prince Malcolm had when she and her parents had gone to visit two years ago. Although . . . now that she found herself in the position of being Luella's pet frog, Imogene realized she was having sudden second thoughts about the whole keeping-an-animal thing.

Luella gave it one more try. "I brought my best dress," she said, indicating what she was wearing. "For *acting* in."

Imogene felt bad she had not noticed that Luella had changed. The dress was faded and frayed, though not so badly as her everyday dress. And Luella had combed her hair. Unlike Imogene, Luella had *great* hair.

"Very pretty," Imogene told her. Too late.

Luella finished by saying, rather lamely, "Bertie said you got crowns and tiaras and necklaces and such—made from wood but painted to look like gold and rubies and emeralds. He said maybe I could wear one."

Ned gestured toward the chests in the cart. "Yours for the choosing," he said. "Just be careful not to chip the paint while you're making supper."

"I . . ." Luella started.

Imogene could read on the farm girl's face the words that were on the tip of her tongue. She was about to say: *I hate you.*

But she restrained herself. She turned and stomped away.

"Well," Ned said to Imogene, "that didn't go nearly half badly."

"You're mean," Imogene told him. "And I'm not a frog."

Ned cocked his head and put on a theatrical "thinking" expression.

"Well, yes, all right, I am a frog," Imogene conceded, "but—"

"Be that as it may," Ned interrupted, "it's to everyone's best interests for you to behave. Are you ready?"

With no idea what to expect, Imogene admitted, "I don't know."

"Just follow my lead."

Ned picked up a stool from the back of the cart and brought it into the village square, where he set it in front of a group of waiting children. Sitting himself down, Ned placed Imogene on his knee. He spoke loudly, obviously for the benefit of the children and for the adults beyond them. "Well, my little green friend. Here we are in another village." He asked one of the children, "What's the name of this place?"

"St. Eoforwic," several of them replied.

"St. Eoforwic," Ned repeated. To Imogene, he asked, "So what do you think of the fine village of St. Eoforwic?" Before she could wonder what in the world he wanted her to answer, he held her up to his ear as though to hear a whispered reply. "Oooh," he said. "Really? Well, I think so, too. Uh-huh . . . uh-huh . . . Oh, yes, definitely much better than Swinburn, where we were yesterday. What do you like best about it? Hmm . . . you know, I do believe I must agree with you . . ."

This struck Imogene as rather pointless, as he could do the same thing with a regular non-speaking frog. Or a rock, for that matter.

By this point, the children were laughing and calling out things like "That's a frog, mister!" as though maybe Ned didn't know. And "Frogs can't talk!" Until one very little girl complained, "I can't hear nothing!"

Ned told them, "Well, you see, my frog is a little bit shy. She doesn't like to talk when there's a whole big crowd of people. That's why she whispers in my ear."

Several of the older children hooted. The parents looked on indulgently.

Imogene hoped that when Ned wanted her to do something, he'd give her a clear signal.

Ned crooked his finger at the little can't-hear-nothing girl to come closer. "But maybe for you, because you're such a sweet, pretty little girl, she might speak to someone besides me. Go on, tell her your name."

Although Ned held Imogene up to the girl's ear, the girl assumed the question was for her. "Wilda," she said.

Being a clever actor, Ned was never at a loss for something to say. He said to Imogene, "Say hello to Wilda."

And that, Imogene guessed, was her signal. She whispered to the girl, "Hello, Wilda."

The little girl's eyes grew wide with amazement. "She did! She said it! She said, 'Hello, Wilda.'"

The other children laughed at Wilda, and one or two called her a fool.

"Well, that's not very kind," Ned told the crowd. "It looks as though people don't believe me *or* Wilda." To Imogene, he said, "I suspect you're going to have to speak louder, or poor Wilda will get a reputation for being a bit off in the head." He held Imogene up high in his hand.

Which was as clear a signal as Imogene could hope for. She cleared her throat and loudly announced, "I said: 'Hello, Wilda.'"

The villagers gasped appreciatively and clapped.

"And what's your name?" Ned asked.

Did he want her to say? Well, if he didn't want her to, he should have told her what to say instead. "I am Princess Imogene Eustacia Wellington. I have been kidnapped by these people and am being held against my will."

Cheers, and more clapping.

Which was definitely not the reaction she had been hoping for.

"Really," she said. "I am your princess, turned into a frog by a witch."

The people clearly thought this was all part of the performance. Several shouted out, "We don't got a princess," and "All we got is Prince Durwin," and "He ain't a frog—he's more like a rabbit."

This was worse than Imogene had thought. They were already so far beyond the border of her father's kingdom that nobody here had even heard of her.

Ned regained control of the crowd by telling them, "Princess Imogene Eustacia Wellington is princess of . . . *the Frog Pond.*"

"Ahh," the people said, as though that made any sense.

"And," he continued, "Princess Imogene Eustacia Wellington has just told me that she is totally charmed by this little village of . . . What was it again?"

It was no use fighting him and getting him peeved with her. "St. Eoforwic," Imogene said.

The crowd loved that.

Ned continued, "And what Princess Imogene Eustacia Wellington whispered in my ear before is that she believes it's the most excellent village we've visited yet."

People applauded.

"And that the best thing is the people, who are so kind. Isn't that right, Princess Imogene Eustacia Wellington?"

"Very kind," Imogene agreed. She didn't add, *Though somewhat dense.* How could they believe she was a talking frog? Yet the adults were murmuring things like "Well, I never!" and "What will they think of next!" It was like a whole village of Luellas.

"And," Ned said, raising his voice to be heard above the appreciative murmurings, "and not only can this very clever frog speak, but it speaks several different languages."

Softly, for only Ned to hear, Imogene said, "Regardless of what Luella and Bertie believe, I am not a Chinese speaking frog. I do not speak Chinese."

Ned just smiled. He said to the villagers, "Princess Imogene Eustacia Wellington of"—he paused for emphasis—"the Frog Pond . . . can speak . . . cat. Princess?"

Unenthusiastically, Imogene said, "Me-oww."

"And dog."

How embarrassing. "Bow-wow."

"And pig."

"Oink."

"And even rooster."

Imogene looked at Ned levelly. "You are joking," she said.

But the crowd laughed harder at this than they had at the other animals.

"Cock-a-doodle-doo," Imogene said.

Looking well pleased with how the act had gone, Ned swept to his feet and bowed. Which must have been the signal for the other actors to walk amongst the crowd with their hats held out for coins. By the chinking, they collected a lot of coins. "My frog and I appreciate your kindness. And we hope you enjoy the rest of the show. Princess Imogene Eustacia Wellington?"

"Enjoy," she echoed hollowly.

Now she understood. Ned knew she was a princess, but he figured he could make more money by showing her as a talking frog than he could by returning her to her parents.

How would she ever get home?

Chapter 9

A Princess Is Loyal to Her Friends in Need

(Except, of course, when she isn't)

The performance consisted of various acts of juggling, tumbling, and magic. Imogene was able to watch while she kept Luella company in the back of the cart as Luella prepared vegetables for a stew that would be supper for those whose diet consisted of more than bugs on the wing.

The only thing remotely resembling acting was when Ned recited a long poem. A long, long, *long* poem. Imogene counted twenty-seven stanzas—and she only started counting after she already thought it had gone on forever. In all honesty, she felt the reciting was decently well done, with Ned's voice alternately going loud and soft, slow and fast, angry and tearful, but she suspected Ned was the author of the piece, and—based on this—she judged he would do better to stick to acting.

When it was all over—not only the poem finished, but the crowd dispersed, the money counted, the costumes returned to the cart (folding was another of Luella's jobs, it turned out), and the actors assembled for dinner—Imogene gathered from the men's good humor that they considered this a better-than-average night.

"It was a good show," Luella acknowledged to Ned. She hesitated before handing his bowl to him, so that he was forced to look directly at her. "You and the frog. I paid attention. I can do it tomorrow."

Imogene bobbed her head in agreement, the closest she could come to nodding with her basically neckless frog anatomy.

Ned gazed heavenward, either for patience or for the right words. "I do not judge the act to be quite ready yet for the understudy," he told the two of them. But then, before Luella could start hurling ladlefuls of the stew, he added, "What we will be doing tomorrow as we travel is learning the lines for the play we will perform the day after. And as for the play, my lovely Luella, yours will be the key role: our success will be dependent upon you."

Luella went from looking as though she wanted to strangle Ned to looking as though she might hug him. "Oh!" she exclaimed, her voice brimming over with happiness. But a moment later, a dab of suspicion crept in. "Do you really mean it? Is there a part for me?"

"The play," Ned told her, "is one of my own devising. It is called: *The Valiant Adventures of King Rexford the Bold and How He Rescued the Beauteous and Virtuous Queen Orelia from the Underground Halls of the Evil Dwarf Lord Stoc of the Red Talons.*"

"Oooo," Luella said, somewhat breathlessly.

"Oooo," Imogene echoed. Then she added, "So is there more to the story, or do you just recite that title?"

Ned must have caught that Imogene was not as impressed as she should have been, and he was clearly peeved at her question. He announced, "If one is implying that the title is overlong, one is incorrect. Since this is a story with which most people will—at this point in time—be unfamiliar, the title must hint at the tone and content of the play while simultaneously whetting their appetites. It is a play in five acts, told in poetical form—in iambic pentameter to be exact, with the occasional heroic couplet. The company has had good experience presenting this story. It makes the audience weep; it makes them laugh; it makes their brains ache from opening up to thoughts they never had before."

"Oooo," Luella said again.

Imogene asked, "And your answer to Luella's question about whether there's a part for her is . . . ?"

"My dear girl . . ." Ned said. He stopped to consider, then he corrected that to " . . . frog . . ." Then he recorrected that to " . . . girl frog . . ."

Imogene yawned.

Ned said, "The incomparable Luella has been my muse, my source of inspiration for expanding the part of Queen Orelia, from a supporting role to"—he opened his arms dramatically—"being included in the very title."

This was so different from what Imogene had expected that she was left with nothing else to say.

Which worked out well, for Luella spent the next several moments squealing in excitement and happiness. In fact, she was so pleased, she even agreed to wash the costumes the following day, so that they would be in readiness for the performance.

When that following morning came, Imogene sat by the river while Luella laundered the clothes that the actors would wear for the play, which—in the interest of saving time—they referred to as "King Rex." Not "Queen Orelia," Imogene noted, despite Ned's assurances that the play was nothing without her. But, since Ned also kept reminding the actors, "Timing is everything," Imogene took this advice to heart and decided it would be best to keep her doubts to herself for now.

"Isn't this the most lovely gown you ever seen?" Luella asked Imogene, holding up Queen Orelia's dress.

Not knowing what to say, Imogene fell back on "Rrr-bitt," because she didn't want to point out that the fabric was rather thin to begin with, now grown threadbare from many wearings; the seams were sloppily sewn; and the gems that decorated the bodice were made of thin pieces of painted wood and slivers of metal. The dress Imogene wore under her skin of frog, even though it was one of her older day-to-day dresses, was, in fact, finer.

Luella said, "I need to take the hem up on account of the last person to play this part must of been taller than me. And maybe nip it in at the waist a bit."

But before Luella could get too carried away with her plans, Ned called over to her to hurry up because they had a long distance to travel that day, and there was no time for her to dawdle.

And tomorrow, Imogene thought, *we'll be in Balton Keep, and I'll have word sent to the king, and finally—finally!—I'll get to go back home. And somehow or other, Father will find a way to get me back into my own body.* Her own body—even her own habitually unruly hair—was looking better and better to Imogene.

As the company of actors walked—or, in the case of Imogene, rode on Luella's shoulder—Ned told them the story of the play, taking on the roles of each of the characters and reciting many of the most stirring lines, with much dramatic waving of the arms and striking of heroic poses. There seemed to be quite a few sword fights, Imogene thought, some clever wordplay, and—in her opinion—at least one too many declarations of undying love.

And all of this was without apparent thought given to *why* the characters were doing much of what they did. But maybe some of the lines that Ned *didn't* recite filled in those gaps. Imogene couldn't think of any excuse for the bad poetry.

Ned's declared philosophy was to have all the actors learn all the parts, so that they could play them interchangeably. This not only allowed for last-moment substitutions in case of sore throats or other indispositions, he explained, but over the years he had seen that with everyone knowing the play so thoroughly, there would be fewer cases of missed cues and losing track of one's lines.

The three older actors had performed this play before. Bertie had not, but he knew how to read, and Ned gave him pages to memorize. Luella did not know how to read, so various of the actors took turns feeding her lines.

"It don't make no sense for me to learn the men's lines," Luella protested. "That's just plain silliness. And there's *so* many lines of my own to remember as Queen Orelia."

"All the same . . ." Ned told her.

"And I'm worried that Orelia is a bit . . . oh, I don't

know . . ." Luella hesitated, and Imogene finished for her, "slow to catch on to things," just as Ned provided the word "innocent."

"I mean," Luella pressed, "how can she not see that the evil dwarf king is . . . you know . . . evil?"

Imogene couldn't resist adding, "Not to mention . . . a dwarf."

"That will be taken care of when I block out where everyone is to stand," Ned assured them. "Orelia is trusting, and that just points to her goodness."

"Oh," Luella said.

"Hmm," Imogene said.

Both *slow to catch on to things* and *trusting* sounded just as much like Luella as the fictional Queen Orelia. Imogene couldn't help but think that was what Ned meant when he said Luella had inspired him. She didn't think Luella would be pleased.

Luella continued to be trusting through their arrival in the town of Mayfield that evening, where Ned and Imogene performed an act very similar to the one they had done in St. Eoforwic—except that in this case, *Mayfield* was the most excellent village they had ever visited and had the kindest people.

And Luella continued to be trusting while her only job in Mayfield was to do the marketing before, and to lead the applause for the performers during, and to cook and clean up after the men did their acts.

And she continued to be trusting through the following day as everyone once more practiced all the lines of the play while they traveled to the bigger town of Balton Keep.

But that trust cracked open and disappeared when the actors went to put on their costumes for the play.

Imogene was swimming in the big cauldron, which was sitting in the back of the cart, when Luella frantically asked her, "Have you seen it? I can't find my dress. Oh my goodness! I didn't leave it back by the stream where I washed it, did I?" Luella flung shirts and prop crowns and various hats and wigs out of her way as she looked through the chest where she'd already looked twice. "I must have!" Luella wailed. "It's well and truly gone! Oh, Ned will be furious with me for losing it!"

Imogene noticed that Luella was more worried about

what Ned would have to say than how Bertie would re-act—the exact opposite of the way things had been when this journey had begun. But she didn't point that out; she just reassured Luella, "You couldn't have left the dress at the stream. You were working on the hem last night."

This observation didn't calm Luella one bit. "Then I must have left it in Mayfield," she groaned. "Oh, what will we do? How will people ever know I'm supposed to be a queen if I'm wearing my own drab dress instead of a costume?"

"Luella!" Imogene said sharply, trying to bring the farm girl back to her senses. "The dress was on top of the pile of costumes. You've been opening the chest to look at it all afternoon. It must be here."

Luella took in a deep breath. "Someone must of stoled it!" she said with a gasp. "It's the only explanation."

But it wasn't the only explanation.

For in another moment, Bertie joined them, and he was wearing the costume dress, as well as a wig of long, light brown hair and a crown. "I can't believe this," Bertie was complaining, tugging at the waist to give himself more breathing room. "How could I have gained so much around my middle since the last time I wore this? And I must have grown taller, too. This just plain doesn't fit anymore."

Here we go, Imogene thought. But she had no joy in it.

"Bertie!" Luella said. She tried to force a laugh, as though Bertie had put on the dress as a joke. "Bertie, what're you doing, wearing my costume?"

Bertie looked up from pulling at the dress. "It's my costume," he said.

"No, it's not," Luella told him.

"Yes, it is," Bertie corrected her.

Luella stamped her foot. "You said you were the lead actor."

Bertie raised his voice, to match Luella's increasing volume. "And I am. I am the lead actor of the female roles. As the youngest actor in this troupe, I am the one best suited to the work of portraying females."

Luella kicked him. "But I *am* a female. I could play the female roles better."

"Women aren't actors."

"I practiced the lines."

"To help us learn ours."

"Ned!" Luella called.

"Ned!" Bertie shouted.

"Ned!" Imogene croaked, because—though she hated to see Luella's feelings hurt—this seemed like a changing point for everyone.

Ned came to see what was the problem, wearing the robes of King Rexford the Bold. (*Of course* Ned would give himself the part with the most lines, Imogene thought.) "Oh," he said as soon as he saw Luella glaring at Bertie wearing the queen's costume.

Luella positioned herself directly in front of Ned, with her hands on her hips, and her voice quivering with anger. "You said," she told him, "that I would play the part of Queen Orelia."

"No, I did not," Ned answered, calmly for all that Luella was within range to spit at, kick, or throttle him. "I said that you had inspired me in my reconceiving of the character."

Imogene spoke up in Luella's defense. "You *implied*."

Luella nodded in acknowledgment of Imogene's support, then spoke through clenched teeth, telling Ned, "You said—"

"And," Ned hurriedly added, talking over her, "I said

that you would play a key role, the most important role to our success."

"And what role would that be?" Luella demanded.

Ned stepped closer to the cart. And surely, Imogene thought, it wasn't coincidence that this moved him farther from Luella. His hand hovered over the various painted crowns, tiaras, and jewelry that Luella had cast aside in her search through the costumes for Queen Orelia's dress. He settled on a necklace with painted enamel beads that Imogene could only suppose were meant to be sapphires, if you stood far enough away, and he draped this around Luella's neck. "Beautiful," he murmured. "This piece brings out the blue of your eyes. Would you like a crown, too? I think a crown would suit you."

Luella pushed his hand away before he could set the crown on her head. "Who am I playing?" she asked.

"Who?" Ned repeated. Then switched that to "Whom?" apparently unable to stop himself from correcting the farm girl's grammar. "Well, I wouldn't so much say it's a case of *whom* . . ."

"Who am I playing?" Luella shouted at him.

"Since we will all be on the stage—" Ned started.

Imogene cut in by saying, "And by *we*, I take it you mean *the actors* . . ."

Ned hesitated, as though weighing whether there was a safe answer to that. He glanced back and forth between Luella and Imogene. "The men, yes," he admitted, "we need *someone*"—he gestured to indicate Luella—"to pass among the crowd with the hat."

"For the donations," Bertie added, entirely unnecessarily. "In recognition of our performance."

"Because," Ned finished, "crowds are notorious for dispersing as soon as the last lines are spoken, precisely to avoid paying for the entertainment they've just enjoyed. But for a pretty girl like you, smiling and winking at the men, they will be willing to part with a coin or two and consider themselves the richer for it."

"Smiling and winking?" Imogene croaked, outraged on Luella's behalf.

Really, though, Luella was outraged enough on her own. She shouted, "You lied to me!"

"I never did," Ned insisted. "Of course, I don't know what Bert might have said to you . . ."

Bertie squirmed before finally admitting, "In my eagerness to have you join us . . ." He thought better of this. ". . . me—to have you join *me*—I might have . . . perhaps the word I'm looking for is *overstated* . . . a bit . . . the extent to which Ned was likely to allow you to participate . . . Maybe."

"And," Ned said, "I did warn you that an actor's word was not to be trusted."

"You're all pigs!" Luella told them.

Imogene felt a little swinish herself, since she had suspected just such an outcome and had not warned Luella. *But she wouldn't have believed me,* Imogene told herself. Still, her voice came out very little as she reminded Luella, "I'm not a pig. I'm a frog."

"Yes!" Ned said, obviously relieved for the break in the awkward moment. "So you are! You most assuredly are! And we must do something about that."

This should have sounded like good news, but somehow Imogene doubted it was. "What do you mean?" she asked.

"We must make you look like a crow."

"Excuse me?" Imogene said.

"I've written in a part for you. You are to play the messenger crow of Stoc, the wizard dwarf. You will be a sensation!"

Luella squealed, "She gets to be in the play, but I don't? She don't even want to be an actor! She wants to be a princess."

"Be that as it may," Ned told Luella, "you, my dear, would never pass as a crow."

"Neither would I!" Imogene cried.

"Trust me," Ned said, which was highly unlikely, given the circumstances.

Imogene became aware that Luella was looking at her in anger and revulsion.

"How could you?" Luella demanded, and she turned and walked away from all of them.

"I . . ." Imogene said, "I . . ."

Watching Luella stomp away, Ned said to Bertie, "She didn't take the hat. Is she going to take the hat around, or isn't she?"

"I don't know," Bertie admitted.

Ned called after Luella, "Feel free to wear the necklace while you're passing the hat. But you can leave it here when you're finished." Still, he said to Bertie, "I don't think she's going to pass the hat. She took the necklace, and she's not going to give it back."

"It's just a cheap fake," Imogene told him. "And so are you."

"Ouch," Ned said, but not very convincingly. He gave a smile that Imogene was certain any nine out of ten people would find charming. "Let's go over your lines."

Chapter 10

A Princess Should Know How to Dress Properly for Every Occasion

(So, what's the proper dress for improper occasions?)

$\mathcal{I}$ mogene's costume was a knitted coin pouch.

A coin pouch.

Life on the stage can be SO humiliating, Imogene thought.

Already Ned's decision to have her perform in the play had cost her the one friend that she'd currently had in the world—even if Luella could only be accounted as a temporary, sort-of friend. Now there was this pouch. The costume element came from a bunch of feathers stuck into the unimaginative brown lump of yarn. In addition to the fancy plumes borrowed from the hats in the costumes chest—one each of pheasant, ostrich, and peacock—were ones Ned had picked up as they walked: Imogene recognized starling and sparrow. And one that might, by purest chance, actually be crow. Two of the feathers had their shafts bent and angled and placed in such a way as to look like wings.

Assuming that a crow could have such skimpy wings.

And that one wing could be gray and the other brown and black striped.

Ned backed Imogene into the feathery pouch, then tugged on the drawstring so that the material puckered around and framed her face—the only part of her that showed. Even then, she had to hold on to the edge with her tiny frog fingers to keep the opening positioned in front of her face and to keep from disappearing entirely into the sack.

"Perfect!" he exclaimed.

"Perfectly ridiculous," Imogene countered. "Why do I have to be a messenger crow? Why can't I be a messenger frog?"

"Because *frog* doesn't rhyme with *know* and *snow*."

"What?" Imogene snapped.

Ned recited:

"Tell unto the king, for he needs must know,
no friends survive for to rescue him now.
Dead they lie, scattered about the meadow,
their blood like rosebuds n'er destined to bloom,
beneath the cover of the new fall'n snow.
You are alone, my king—they cannot come.
Fly, fly, and tell him thus, my faithful crow."

Imogene repeated the lines in her head. "It could be *fog* instead of *snow*," she pointed out.

"No, it couldn't," Ned answered, obviously horrified at the suggestion.

"But, yes, listen." Imogene stood as tall as a frog wearing a wig of feathers could and recited:

" . . . beneath the cover of the creeping fog . . .
Fly, fly, and tell him thus, my faithful frog."

"That makes no sense," Ned objected.

"As much sense as your version."

Ned looked appalled that anyone could say such a thing.

Imogene continued, "And my way helps that one line about the new fallen snow, where there are too many syllables."

"That's why it's new *fall'n* snow," Ned said, swallowing the last syllable of *fallen*.

Imogene opened her mouth to protest some more, but Ned cut her off. "I am the writer," he told her. "You are the actor."

"I," she corrected him, "am the frog who is being made to look ridiculous." She thought about that for a moment, realized what she'd just said, and changed that to "the *princess* who is being made to look ridiculous." She once more mentally ran through the lines, then added, "But surely those words are spoken *to* the crow, not *by* the crow?"

Ned inclined his head in agreement. "They are spoken by Stoc, the dwarf lord."

"And do I answer?"

"No. But four scenes later you deliver the message. You must remember to speak slowly, loudly, and to enunciate, so that even those in the back rows can hear." Looking well pleased with himself, Ned declaimed:

"Lord Stoc of the talons, your greatest foe,
has sent you this message for you to hear:
Those who would save you lie dead in the snow,
their blood like rosebuds n'er destined to bloom,
beneath the cover of the new fall'n snow.
You are alone, my king—they cannot come.
Thus I have spoken, his messenger crow."

When it became clear there was no more, Imogene said, "That's it? That's just a reworking of what Stoc said."

Apparently, Ned knew this already. "Well, yes, the messenger crow has been sent to deliver a message. That is, in fact, why it is called a *messenger* crow and not a *why-don't-you-go-visit-the-king-and-tell-him-whatever-your-little-crow-heart-desires* crow."

"You don't need to raise your voice," Imogene told Ned. "I understand what you're saying from a *messenger* point of view. I'm just saying that—from a *play* point of view—does the audience want to hear the same thing it's already heard before?" Imogene thought she was being tactful with his writerly feelings by not saying "the same foolish thing," but apparently this wasn't enough.

"Just say the lines the way I've written them," Ned snapped. "*I* will decide if and when they need to be changed. You're just lucky I could think of *any* part for you."

He'd written the role specifically for her, Imogene knew. The crow had been mentioned before—a necessary plot device to explain how King Rexford knew not to wait for the men he had sent for at the end of act two—but the crow had never actually appeared before. How could it have? Ned could never have dreamed he'd have someone on hand who was the right size to play a crow.

Still, *lucky* wasn't the word that came to Imogene's mind.

But she did start to feel as though things might be looking up when Ned told her he wanted the people of Balton Keep to see her up close—and without her silly costume, thank goodness—before her debut in the play, so that they could truly appreciate that she wasn't just a trick of stagecraft. People who could be expected to know about stagecraft was a good sign. They would be a more sophisticated group than the farmers and few tradespeople of St. Eoforwic and Mayfield. They wouldn't easily swallow a story about a frog who was—as Ned always said so dramatically—Princess of the Frog Pond, and who just happened to know how to talk.

While Imogene doubted King Salford or his queen would come to a performance such as theirs, at the very least she could expect him to hear about it and to recognize her name. He might question the idea of a frog who claimed to be the stolen-away princess of a neighboring realm—especially if news of her disappearance had reached here.

In any case, it was the best chance she'd had since Luella and Bertie had made off with her. So she started out hopeful when, once more, Ned gathered in a crowd by chatting with the local children.

As ever, Ned talked to Imogene, then held her up to his ear for her "answers," until some child—this time it was a sweet little boy who almost broke Imogene's heart by reminding her so much of her little brother, Will—complained that he couldn't hear.

"Come closer, Tom," Ned said once he'd found out the child's name, and then he held Imogene up so that she could whisper, "Hello, Tom."

But this time, after the child proclaimed that the frog

did, indeed, talk, Ned interrupted the hooting of the older children by saying, "Now, let me tell you something about my frog. This is not an ordinary frog—as Tom here can attest. For, as you fine people have so rightly indicated"—he held his arm out to include them all—"frogs can't talk. Absolutely. You are entirely correct. What an outstanding audience."

The change was a little one, the kind Ned called "a tweaking," and disconcerting only because it came so close to where she was normally called on to start speaking. Imogene waited for him to work his way back to the part she knew.

Ned asked, "So how can my frog talk? Well, let me tell you: He's no ordinary frog."

He? Imogene's tiny frog eardrums quivered. *What?*

But her eardrums were downright vibrating when Ned leaned forward and told them, "He's a prince."

What?

"His name is Jack."

WHAT?

Ned said, "So, now, my fine people, you tell me: How would a prince like Jack turn into a frog?"

And all the younger children and quite a few of the older ones shouted, "Witch!" and "Magic!" and "Magical spell!"

Then, finally—finally—Ned turned back to Imogene and said, "Tell the people your full name, Prince Jack."

Imogene stamped her foot. "I am not Prince Jack. I am Princess Imogene Eustacia Wellington."

The crowd howled.

"Oh dear," Ned said. "It sounds as though being turned into a frog has gotten Prince Jack confused about quite a few things."

Even more laughter.

"I am not Jack!" Imogene said in her loudest croak. "I am not a boy! This man has kidnapped me and stolen me from my home. My parents, King Wellington and Queen Gloriane, will give a great reward to anyone who returns me to them. Tell King Salford about me!"

Was there ever a more appreciative audience? The more she shouted that King Salford must be told, the more the audience cheered.

Until, finally, without even doing the bit about talking like other animals, Ned took pity on her—or, more likely, decided to leave the crowd while they were still wildly enthusiastic for more. He told them, "Pay heed during our play. Prince Jack has a small but important part in act three." As Ned carried her back to the cart while the other actors dispersed among the crowd with outstretched hats, she heard some of those adults who knew about stagecraft asking each other, "How did they do that?" And the answer was . . .

"He must be one of them new ventriloquy artists."

Imogene covered her face and moaned. This just kept getting worse and worse.

There was still no sign of Luella, but the other actors continued to collect coins from the crowd, who were eager to show their appreciation of the act, when Ned set her down in the pot of water. Although this cooled her skin, it did not cool her temper.

"Just for that," she announced, "I am not performing in your play."

"Don't pout and be unpleasant," Ned told her. "They wouldn't have believed you anyway. I just made things more entertaining."

"You made me look like a crazy person."

"Well . . ." Ned actually had a pleasant laugh—except that he was laughing at her. " . . . maybe a crazy frog . . ."

"That's not funny."

"Still," Ned said, "you must perform. Otherwise I might have to drain the water from this pot and leave you to grow dry. What would that gain either of us?"

Imogene climbed onto her rock, then dove off, intentionally splashing him.

It wasn't that big a splashing, and Imogene caused no damage to Ned's King Rex costume. Ned told her, "I'll take that as a disgruntled acceptance of my terms."

Imogene kept swimming and refused to answer.

Suddenly a shadow fell over her, like a cloud passing across the sun. Only it wasn't a cloud, it was a scarf—and Ned was positioning it to cover the opening of the cauldron. Seeing her noticing him, Ned said, "I am aware that your promise to not try to escape was given to Luella. And that you might perhaps no longer feel bound to that promise since dear Luella no longer graces our company. This is just a little safeguard until we come to our own arrangement, you and I."

Imogene was so very angry, she decided that she'd be foolish not to try anything she could. "I agree," she said.

Ned quirked an eyebrow at her.

"Shall we kiss to seal the arrangement?" she asked.

Ned tipped his head—looking at her. Evaluating. Considering.

Imogene's breath caught. She hadn't really expected this might work. Could it? Possibly?

Instead of fastening the scarf, Ned reached into the water and held her in the palm of his hand. For the first time in days, she let herself dare to hope.

Ned looked directly into her eyes. Then, again, gave his low, throaty laugh. "Not a chance," he told her.

Cuella still had not returned by the time the play started, and Imogene guessed that was final proof the farm girl must be well and truly gone.

"Don't you miss her?" she asked Bertie, as he plopped Imogene into her costume and drew it up so that only her face showed.

Bertie, great sentimentalist that he had turned out to be, said, "The play must go on."

For all that it seemed overwrought and overwritten to Imogene, *The Valiant Adventures of King Rexford the Bold and How He Rescued the Beauteous and Virtuous Queen Orelia from the Underground Halls of the Evil Dwarf Lord Stoc of the Red Talons* appeared to be going well. The stage was actually just a clearing in the middle of the square. Scaffolding that could be rotated and that was draped with various gauzy fabrics stood in for walls to indicate the changing scenes. The crowd cheered every time King Rexford appeared, booed every time the dwarf Lord Stoc came on, and whistled and yelled, "Nice ankles!" at Bertie as Queen Orelia, wearing the noticeably too tight, too short dress.

Imogene had to be in all those scenes that took place in the dwarves' underground citadel, even though she had no lines for the first two acts. She just sat in the birdcage that hung from a bracket that was fastened to the scaffolding. In her first scene, she heard several of the children call and point her out. ("Look, it's the frog! It's the frog that thinks it's a princess, pretending to be a bird!") Which was sweet, even if in an annoying sort of way, and made her want to please the children. Even though all four of her feet were encased in the feathery pouch, she managed to give a little hop, which she thought a caged crow might do. But apparently the actor who was playing Lord Stoc thought that distracted the audience from *his* lines at the time, and when next he passed close to her cage, he hissed at her, "Stay to the script!"

Then came act three.

Bertie—who didn't have much to do in the third act, and so was helping behind the scenes—came up and tied a string to what, previously, Imogene had thought was just a loose bit of thread in her costume. Now she suddenly realized there were two loops, one under each of her wings, and that certainly looked intentional.

"What's this?" she asked.

"Nothing," Bertie assured her.

"What do you mean *nothing?*" She tried to see where the strings he'd just attached to her led, but she could not.

Ned went "*Ssst!*" at her, since two actors were on the other side of the curtains, engaged in a scene.

Bertie placed Imogene in the crow cage, with the strings hanging outside and leading . . . leading . . .

Imogene kept leaning this way and that, trying to determine where the other ends of the string were attached, but Ned went, "*Ssst!*" again, and the town lads who had been hired to turn the scaffolding when needed now picked it up and swiveled it to reveal to the audience the gray curtains that signified "underground."

Imogene's cage was still swaying from the scene change when she realized that Lord Stoc was already delivering his lines to her. He said "fallen snow" instead of "fall'n snow," which gave the line too many beats, and for which Ned would surely rebuke him, since Imogene had heard them specifically discuss this. But then Lord Stoc was saying:

> *"You are alone, my king—they cannot come.*
> *Fly, fly, and tell him thus, my faithful crow."*

Imogene was expecting the scaffolding to be turned again, onto what was supposed to be the forest glade where the next scene took place. Not that anybody had actually told her this would happen. But what else could be done when there was a frog playing the part of a crow?

Except, instead, Lord Stoc flung open the door to the cage.

"What?" Imogene whispered at him.

He mouthed the word *Fly!* at her, then tugged at her dangling strings, which dragged her to the very edge of the cage's opening.

Fly?

And then suddenly Imogene was lifted into the air.

It was sort of like falling—except, of course, without the ultimate release of hitting the ground. Which would have been a relief, compared to the sensation of never-ending hurtling through the air. "Rrr-bitt!" Imogene cried. Obviously, this was not the right thing for a crow to say, even if she hadn't already been warned about not deviating from the script. The strings, she finally saw, were attached to a wooden pole that Bertie, behind the curtain, held: dipping it and swaying it and oh-my-goodness spinning it to simulate flight.

Well, not so much *flight* as bouncing in the air.

The crowd whistled and stamped their feet in appreciation, apparently willing to forgive her startled out-of-character outcry.

Imogene was sure she was going to die. If not from the flying itself, then from the fright. She was sure she didn't breathe once. If she could have closed her eyes, she would have. At the very least, she wanted to let go of the edge of the pouch so that the material would slip up and encase her entirely. That way she wouldn't have to watch. But she couldn't get her froggy fingers to loosen.

Then, finally, the scaffolding was turned, ending Imogene's ordeal.

Ned, standing off to the side, mimed clapping his hands to show that, all in all, he was pleased.

Well, a good thing *somebody* was.

"I hate you!" she croaked.

He pointed to his ear and shrugged to indicate he couldn't hear above the still-cheering crowd.

"We're not going to do that again, are we?" she asked, as Bertie tucked her back into the crow cage for safekeeping until her next scene.

Bertie was too busy fidgeting with his ill-fitting dress to answer.

Or maybe, Imogene thought, he just didn't want to answer.

Because otherwise he probably would have unfastened the strings from the pole.

"Frogs are not meant to fly!" she croaked. But he—and all the other busy actors, too—ignored her.

Sure enough, when Ned was on stage as King Rexford in the tower prison, Bertie came to fetch her. There was a gap in the curtains, signifying a window, and Imogene could guess what was coming next.

She knew it was no use begging for mercy. The most she could do was to tell Bertie, "Easy with the swooping."

"Yes, yes," he said. "I'm a trained professional."

Which might have been more of a consolation if he hadn't tripped over the skirt of his dress as he said it.

"You've pulled the hem out," Imogene observed.

"It was too short. It was distracting to the audience."

"Well, now it's too long. And it's ragged."

"Yes, well . . ." Bertie looked down at the hem. "You don't happen to know how to sew, do you?"

"That's not going to happen," Imogene told him. "Just walk carefully."

Bertie had a bit of advice for her, too. "And you, even though you're speaking your lines to King Rexford, make sure you face outward, toward the audience, or they won't be able to hear you."

And the next thing she knew, she was hoisted into the air and Bertie swung her around into the scene so the audience could see her.

"Yay! It's the frog prince!" the children shouted.

Imogene saw a flicker of displeasure cross Ned's face: annoyance at the disruption. Well, what had he expected, casting a frog in the role of a crow?

Ned spoke the lines of her cue:

> *"Hark! What dark-omened portent can this be?*
> *Could't be mine own death, come looking for me?"*

Even while Imogene winced at the mangling that forced "Could it be" into two syllables, even while she was still soaring through the air, she took a deep breath (it was hard to tell *what* direction she was facing), and—with her voice shaking only a little bit, both for the flying and the acting—she started her own lines:

"Lord Stoc—"

Hiding behind the scaffolding so that he couldn't be seen—but also couldn't see—Bertie sent Imogene smack against the gray curtain below the opening that signified the window. Face first. Which meant she *had* been pointing in the wrong direction. Still, being loose fabric, this was more disorienting than painful—but the curtain *was* supposed to be passing for stonework, so quite a few people in the audience called out comments like "Ow! That must've hurt!"

Spitting out gray threads, still tasting the fabric, Imogene once more started:

"Lord Stoc—"

Bertie raised the pole higher and swung again. On this second try, he got the correct elevation. But went too far. She once more bounced off fabric, this time beyond the so-called window.

The opening of the feathered pouch had shifted sideways, even with her holding on, so that half her face was covered.

Speaking through clenched lips—clenched partly because of annoyance, partly because her little frog stomach was threatening to eject all the flies she'd eaten that day—Imogene said:

"Lord Stoc—"

Somebody toward the front of the audience shouted

out: "In truth, look between the stones of the tower! I do believe I can actually see Death's hand coming for that ill-fated king! And yon poor crow's developed a stutter as well as lost a wing!"

Bertie jerked his arm back out of view—which, of course, sent Imogene soaring even farther from the window, and from the shaken-loose pheasant feather that was meant to pass for a crow wing but was now fluttering earthward.

Enough was enough. Imogene determined to wait until Bertie landed her correctly on the sill of the opening before she'd recite her lines. She was too dizzy to count on remembering them, anyway.

Ned must have decided that the gap needed filling—or that the audience needed reminding of his last line. He had just repeated, "Hark!" when Bertie's improving aim but overly zealous swing sent Imogene through the window opening, hard and fast, directly at Ned's nose. He took a quick step backwards to avoid a faceful of crow-costumed frog, but he had the presence of mind to catch hold of the strings that attached Imogene to the pole so that she dangled, like a snagged mackerel—almost the exact opposite of crow-like—from his fist. He managed to get out, "What dark-omened portent can this be?" before the pole, ripped from Bertie's hand, clattered to the cobblestones of the town square.

There was a moment of stunned silence, during which several more of Imogene's feathers wafted ground-ward.

The silence lasted only until Bertie, off balance, crashed through the scenery.

Though Imogene had not seen her before, she recognized Luella's voice from the audience. Luella, who had stayed after all. She *would have* made a good actor, Imogene thought, for her voice certainly carried: "Oh look! It's the lovely Queen Orelia. Floating like. Dancing. Up by the castle window. It's a miracle!"

The audience whooped and clapped, any mood of heroic drama gone.

And that was before Bertie, still staggering, stepped on his dragging hem and ripped the entire skirt portion off his dress.

And before—trying to keep from falling—he grabbed hold of the scaffolding. And pulled it down with him.

The play was over, and none of the actors even bothered to pass the hat.

Chapter 11

A Princess Watches Out for Others

(Though sometimes others need to watch out for a princess)

Ned handed Imogene, still dangling from the strings attached to her costume, to one of the town lads who had been helping to move the scenery scaffolding. Since that piece of equipment would need quite a bit of reassembling even *if* it was ever to be workable again, the young man might have had grounds to declare his term of employment as having ended; but he agreed to bring her back to the cart and to put her in the cauldron full of water while Ned tried to salvage what he could of the acting troupe's reputation.

The young man carried her, stepping over bits of debris from the scaffolding, and dodging the overripe fruits and vegetables that some from the town were beginning to throw at the stage area. Still encased in her costume/sack, Imogene kicked her back legs, trying to work her way up and out through the opening that was gathered around her face. She had just gotten one front leg free when the man tossed her into the water.

The little sack immediately soaked up enough water that it became too heavy to float. Imogene, still mostly encased in wool and feathers, was dragged down to the bottom.

All right, she thought, *lesson learned: So apparently there are worse things in the world than flying.*

She continued to kick and struggle to get free of the costume, but that did nothing to make her more buoyant and only used up the little bit of air she had in her lungs.

The worst part was that she suspected the lad hadn't done this out of malice; he just wasn't all that bright. It would never have occurred to him to wonder if a frog dressed like a crow might have trouble keeping afloat.

It was bad enough that she was going to die while still in

frog form. But to die as a frog, by drowning, in a crow costume—this was downright embarrassing. It was little consolation that nobody she cared for would ever know.

But just at the moment her froggy lungs protested they could hold her breath no longer, just as she was about to inhale water, a hand reached under her and pulled her soggy self up to the surface. Imogene expected to see the town lad, having realized his mistake and feeling repentant for it. Instead, there stood Luella.

With the mark of true friendship, Luella never commented on the hacking, retching noises Imogene was making, nor complained about the water Imogene coughed up onto her hand. Instead, she only observed, "That's one pitiful costume."

"Absolutely," Imogene managed to gasp out once she was done gagging.

Luella disentangled Imogene from the dripping mass of yarn and feathers. "Still want to go home?" she asked.

And once more Imogene answered, "Absolutely."

Luella tossed both Imogene's crow costume and her own fake sapphire necklace into the cauldron that had formerly been Imogene's home-away-from-home. Then she fetched the pail in which she and Bertie had originally carried Imogene. Although it had been cast aside in the back of the actors' cart, its size and its handle made it portable. She filled it with fresh water, then asked Imogene, "Pail or shoulder?"

"Wait," Imogene said. "Let me think."

She was aware that not many people would be willing to let a frog do their thinking for them and counted herself fortunate that Luella was one of them.

"Shoulder for now," Imogene said. "Which way toward home?"

"West," Luella answered, and she took a step in that direction.

Imogene nodded. "All right. So, what we want to do is make sure people see us heading west."

"Toward home," Luella agreed, also nodding. Then she asked, "Why do we want people to see us?"

"So that they'll tell Ned."

Luella was concentrating so hard she got squinty-eyed. Either that, or she didn't consider this a good plan but didn't want to say so.

On the other hand, Imogene really didn't think Luella could make up her mind that fast. So Imogene explained,

"Except that as soon as we're out of town, we'll circle around to the east, heading *away* from home."

Luella thought about this for a few moments before finally saying, "Which will probably make getting home take longer." But she had caught on, for she finished, "So, Ned and Bertie and them'll assume we've gone home and check that way first and not be able to find us, because we won't be going that way until after we figure they've given up. I had a boyfriend did something like that once when my Da suspected we'd been kissing in the barn and went after him."

Imogene thought, *Of course you did*, but only said, "Right."

And that was how Princess Imogene Eustacia Wellington left the acting life behind and started off home by intentionally heading in entirely the wrong direction.

The rain began soon after they left the town of Balton Keep behind, before they veered off to the east. Then the northeast. Then the east again. Zigzagging. At first, Imogene was pleased, thinking that the hard, steady rain would wash away any tracks of their passing, making finding them harder. *If* anyone wanted to find them. One moment she was sure that Ned would pursue her relentlessly, the next—remembering the broken scaffolding and the foodstuffs the townsfolk had thrown—she wondered if he might not consider the troupe better off without her.

A full day of constant, bone-chilling rain was more than enough, even for a frog who'd spent her first few days worried about becoming too dry. Being wet was nice; getting pelted by raindrops became tiresome. And with the sun hiding deep behind clouds, not only was it sometimes difficult to keep their directions straight, but also there was no way for a cold-blooded frog to get warm, making her drowsy and sluggish, with no energy to keep up with Luella's constant complaining—most of which had to do with how unattractive wet hair looked.

No hair to fret about was perhaps the single advantage Imogene could come up with in being a frog.

They didn't dare stop moving, and they avoided people so that—in case Ned *did* come around asking—there would be no one to say, "Ah, yes! Girl and frog. We saw them yesterday." This meant that they slept outdoors, under the not very rain-proof shelter of some bushes in the woods.

Imogene had more than enough to eat as her frog instincts directed her to all the best places to find bugs hiding out from the rain. Luella had gathered up a few of the more solid vegetables that had been thrown stage-ward in the closing moments of the play, but they were quickly decomposing, and the damp certainly didn't help.

Finally, the second full day, the sun came out. Yay! Except that then everything was hot and steamy. Including Luella's clothing. Which—despite being wet for the past day and a half—could not in any sense be considered washed nor smelling fresh. And apparently humidity was even worse than downright wet as far as Luella's hair was concerned.

What troubled Imogene more was that Luella had developed a sniffle. Imogene wasn't sure if that was from catching a chill that would develop into something worse, or if it was from homesickness. As for herself, Imogene was missing her own family more than she would have ever thought possible: her standoffish mother, her sometimes silly father, her often pesty brother, the regularly scheduled lessons and chores and social obligations that had used to seem such a bother.

"I think," she told Luella—who, if she wasn't ill already,

was definitely on the verge of it, as well as being hungry, worn out, and heartsick—"that we must have put enough distance between ourselves and pursuit."

"All right." Luella didn't even have the energy to sound particularly pleased at the news. "Does that mean we should turn back now?"

"I *think*," Imogene stressed, "that it means we can stop hiding from people. Or, at least, you can. A girl alone will stand out less than a girl and a frog together. Even if the frog isn't talking."

Of course, Imogene reflected, even with wet hair, a girl as pretty as Luella was going to stand out, with or without a frog.

In the days and nights that they had spent together, they had not discussed the past. Still, while Luella never actually said that she had come to believe Imogene was a princess, she no longer called her "Froggy," and she no longer asked what China was like. The closest she came to admitting that she had been mistaken to trust Bertie was to say, in the middle of nothing, "I think I'm going to swear off men."

Well, Imogene thought, *someone like Bertie will do that to a girl.*

In any case, now Luella only asked, "You won't be talking?"

"I won't be with you," Imogene said. "What you should do is go up to one of these farmhouses and offer to do some light work for your keep today—for better food than that one moldy turnip you have left, and for a dry bed. I'll be fine waiting outside, and I can rejoin you tomorrow morning, when we'll turn toward home."

Luella looked at Imogene long and hard. Long enough for Imogene to grow uneasy. Until finally Luella asked, "You're not planning on leaving without me, are you? Abandoning me?"

It surprised Imogene that the thing she herself was most afraid of turned out to be exactly what Luella was anxious over. "No. I'll be here. I'll wait." She didn't ask, *How's an inexperienced frog ever going to find her way home all on her own?* But she did wonder how Luella viewed the situation, what *her* fears were.

Luella found an elderly couple who needed help because just that morning the wife had twisted her ankle and fallen—arms outstretched to break her fall—into the hearth in their kitchen. Fortunately, the twist, the burn, and the bruising were not so severe as they could have been, but the woman was willing to let Luella eat and spend the night, if Luella agreed to prepare the meals, make the beds, do the washing, tend the chickens, milk the goat, bake the bread, collect and hang to dry the herbs from the garden, fix the leaky thatch, and do all the other day-to-day chores that could not stop just because the farm wife was feeling poorly.

"Sounds perfect," Imogene said.

Luella placed Imogene's bucket where it was unlikely to be noticed or kicked over: behind the house, in the shadow between the wall and the water barrel that stood by the back door. Still, just to be safe, *Imogene's* day consisted of ducking underwater whenever a member of the family happened out the back door. In between that were swims, hops, finding bugs, wondering how she would ever shed her froghood, worrying that she *would* never shed her froghood, missing her family, worrying about her family, wondering if it would be better for her family if she didn't return to them—not if she couldn't go back to her true form—and chatting with Luella every time Luella came out to fetch water.

"The woman is nice," Luella told Imogene. "Very sweet."

"That's good," Imogene said.

"The husband," Luella explained, "is busy working his field."

"I understand," Imogene said. "The growing season doesn't stop for household emergencies. Besides, most men are so incompetent in the kitchen, he'd probably be more hindrance than help."

"And the son," Luella finished, "has just returned home after serving in the king's army, and he ain't decided yet how he'll seek his fortune; but—as you say—men are generally no good in the kitchen, anyway."

"Son?" Imogene echoed. "What son?"

Luella rolled her eyes. "The one who just returned home after serving in the king's army. He's much too clever to settle for being a farmer like his Da, but he don't know yet what he wants to do with his life. He's really smart, Imogene. He's sure to be good at something that will gain him fame and riches."

Imogene was ready to knock her little green head against the rock in her pail. "Just as a guess," she said, "does this son happen to be good-looking?"

Luella, who had appeared so pasty and drawn such a

short while ago, flushed and smiled shyly and said, "Why, yes. I suppose he is."

"I thought you'd given up on men," Imogene reminded her. "Men like, for example, Bertie?"

"I *have*," Luella assured her. But she fluffed her hair as she said it. "I need to go back in now to check the kettle I left on the fire."

Imogene tried to console herself. How much trouble could Luella get into in one day?

But the following morning, Luella announced that the woman was feeling even stiffer than before, and that she'd asked Luella to stay on for a bit.

It was pretty boring for Imogene for one day.

Very boring for two days.

Mind-numbingly boring for three.

Especially with the suspicion that the woman wasn't the main reason Luella wanted to extend her stay—suspicion strengthened by the fact that Luella made fewer and fewer trips to the rain barrel, and shorter ones, and always seemed in a rush to get back into the house. The house from which Imogene seemed to be hearing a lot of laughter and good cheer.

Imogene started to wonder if there was any time limit to the froggifying spell beyond which she would no longer be able to turn back to human but would be bound into frog shape forever. There was no real reason to believe so. However, neither was there a strong reason to believe not. Did it mean anything that the old witch responsible for this whole mess hadn't said anything about a need to either rush or be doomed?

Imogene thought back. And decided that, with the old witch, one couldn't assume anything.

I could, she thought, *kiss someone, anyone, for just a bit. Trade places for maybe a few hours.*

A day at the most.

Only until I get back home.

Then I'd change him back.

Really.

Really I would.

But that was dangerous thinking.

And unworthy of a princess.

Finally the old woman was able to get along on her own. At last!

Luella told Imogene, "The son has invited me to stay."

Oh no! Imogene wanted to yell at her. Maybe shake her for good measure. *Oh no! Oh no! Oh no!*

Instead, she spoke very calmly through her frog lips. "I need to get home. Please, Luella, I have no other way of getting there except through your goodwill. Truly, I am Princess Imogene, King Wellington's daughter, regardless of what Bertie said. If you take me to my parents, they will give you whatever you want. They can easily have you brought back here afterward. Please, Luella, don't leave me to try to get home on my own."

Luella picked up Imogene's bucket. "I wouldn't," she said. "I told him no. I know my parents will lecture me until I'm gray and toothless for running off with Bertie, but the fact is I miss them. And my wretched little brother, too. And our farm. So I'm thinking: Why should I always be the one expected to leave my family and friends and go off with *him?* Surely there's got to be a *him* who's willing to come to me."

And that was how Princess Imogene Eustacia Wellington and Luella the farm girl once more took to the road—this time heading west, well and truly traveling toward home.

It took days, as Imogene had known it would, until finally, finally, she saw the very tip of the turret at the northeast corner of the castle, the turret that—through some miscalculation of her great-grandfather's master builder—had somehow ended up just a bit taller than the rest, so that it was always the first anybody saw, no matter from which direction they approached.

Imogene counted up the days since all of this had started. Fourteen. She'd been away fourteen days.

Which meant that, by purest happenstance, she'd come home on her birthday.

She remembered her mother handing her that book, *The Art of Being a Princess*, and telling her that there was just enough time to read it—a chapter a day—before her birthday. Wryly Imogene thought, *And I haven't read a single chapter—just the foreword.*

Still, all in all, she doubted that even her mother could find fault with that now—not under the circumstances.

That was what she was thinking about when a familiar voice said, in ringing, slightly over-enunciated tones so that even the back rows could hear: "Hello, Luella. Hello, Princess Imogene. The troupe wasn't the same without you."

Chapter 12

A Princess Is Never at a Loss for Words

(Blah blah blah blah blah)

Ned sat on the large rock by the side of the road that led to the town and the castle beyond. The rock had been left there by those who had built the road, a place for travelers to rest while getting a drink of water from the stream that was the runoff from the mill pond, or to catch their breath before climbing the final hill.

Imogene found *she* needed to catch her breath, even though she had been riding on Luella's shoulder.

Luella took a step back and glanced around as though gauging which was her best option: to turn and run into the woods and hide; or to throw the pail of water at Ned, then hope she could dart past.

But Ned made no threatening move toward them, nor did he rant and complain that they had abused his hospitality and broken trust with him and cost him money and reputation—as Imogene had imagined these past several days that he might.

He didn't even bother to stand or attempt to appear intimidating. In fact, Imogene thought he looked diminished: both he and his clothing were travel-worn and the worse for the weather since the last time she had seen him. True, *then* he had been wearing the crown and robes of King Rexford the Bold. Of course, he'd also been dodging airborne produce. Still, even with that going on, he'd had his customary bearing of self-importance and confidence. Now he looked mostly weary.

He said, "I told the others that all we had to do was wait. I knew you'd be back."

Imogene didn't say what she thought of the kind of person who couldn't resist an *I told you so*—even to people who were not there. She went directly to "Of course we came back. This is our home. Despite your leading Luella on and kidnapping me."

"Well, of course, obviously you'd eventually *head* toward home," Ned clarified for her. "I meant: I knew you'd make it."

Before Imogene could point out that by acknowledging this as her home, he also acknowledged what and who she was, Ned added, "The troupe has disbanded, which may or may not be all for the best, but however that works out, I found I could not move on until I learned how the story ended."

"Story?" Imogene repeated. "Story? This is my life we're talking about."

Ned shook his head. "Only from your point of view. From mine, you're the lead character in a story that's a better adventure than the ones I've managed to write."

Once again, Imogene refrained from saying the first thing that came to her head: that, in her point of view—in *her* story—he was an irksome, interfering character who kept standing in her way. "In that case," Imogene said, "I'm hoping for a good ending."

"Truly," Ned acknowledged, "I've seen mediocre plays pull things together and thus leave a satisfying impression by a strong ending, and I've seen better plays sunk by a weak ending."

Imogene sighed. "What I was talking about," she clarified, "is a *happy* ending."

"A comedy, then." Ned shrugged, apparently not a fan of comedies. "Tragedies have more staying power than comedies."

"All the same . . ." Imogene said.

"All the same," Ned echoed.

Luella looked from one to the other of them, then declared, "I have no idea what either of you is talking about."

Ned let the subject drop. "As for your getting back home, you're both strong. And capable. Probably more than either of you realizes. And I never kidnapped you, Princess Imogene Eustacia Wellington. I . . . *may* have held on to you longer than I should have. But I never removed you from here." He considered a moment before admitting, "Though I did, perhaps, lead Luella on a bit."

"Perhaps?" Luella sputtered. "A bit?"

"But only after Bert brought you to us. What was I to do? You were glowing with happiness and anticipation that night when you arrived. Was I to inform you then that Bert had deceived you? Tell you that he had exaggerated his importance to the troupe and your importance to him, and that—whatever he'd promised you—he was only using you?" Ned shrugged. Then, despite Imogene's wariness and Luella's obvious distrust of him, he was suddenly on his feet, and he caught hold of Luella's hand.

Imogene's back legs tensed to leap from Luella's shoulder. *I can hide in the woods much more easily alone,* she thought. It wasn't as though she'd be abandoning Luella, for surely Ned was more interested in reclaiming his talking-frog act than in holding on to a farm girl who wanted to be an actor.

But before Imogene could launch herself into the air, all Ned did was bring Luella's hand to his lips. "You can do much better than Bert," he told her.

Luella snatched her hand away. But then she appeared uncertain what to do with it. Her face flushed prettily.

Ned said, "And I *did* try to warn you."

Imogene recalled that he had made a comment to the effect that an actor's word was not to be trusted. Still, she told Ned, "You didn't try very hard."

"I did not," he acknowledged. "But neither did I ever mean Luella harm. And I certainly never meant to permanently hold on to you, Princess Imogene. Just long enough to make . . ." It was his turn to sigh. " . . . a little bit of a sensation. So that people might remember me, and maybe say"—he extended his hands theatrically—"'Now *there* was a showman.'"

"Yes, well," Imogene countered, "you might have held out for: 'Now *there* was someone who rescued a princess in need.'"

Ned nodded. Then pointed out, "Not the same."

"*Not the same,*" Imogene repeated. She studied him. "Please don't tell me, now that I've made it back despite your best efforts to prevent me from doing so, that you plan to tell my parents you held me in safekeeping and so you deserve a reward?"

"I would absolutely know better than to ever tell you that," Ned agreed. "Still, I have to admit: Neither would I duck if someone threw reward money at me. So it's probably best to just switch to a different conversation." He smiled charmingly. "Happy birthday, Princess." He had the grace not to try to kiss her hand.

Not that, strictly speaking, she had a hand.

"How did you know about my birthday?"

"Overheard it. Everyone's frantic about the princess who disappeared practically on the threshold of her thirteenth birthday. No sign of her running off, but no sign of her being carried off, either. And no especial reason to believe in disappearance through mischance. Everyone is stymied. Well"—Ned corrected himself midthought—"I'm guessing not, strictly speaking, *everyone*. I surmise someone must know how you became . . ." He paused to find the proper word. "Frogged? But such a someone no doubt has good enough reason to choose not to come forward."

"Hmm," Imogene said, thinking of the treacherous Harry and the careless witch.

"A world of tantalizing hints in that *hmm*." Ned waited, then continued, "Search parties have looked in every room, in every cupboard, beneath every bed, and behind every dresser, desk, chair, or box in the castle. They've dredged the mill pond—twice—and are even as we speak scouring the woods yet again. Everyone is looking for both of you."

"Both of us?" Luella and Imogene both asked at the same time.

"It didn't escape notice that two girls disappeared the same afternoon. People aren't sure what the connection is, or even if there *is* a connection. But, for the moment, yes: They are looking for both of you."

Luella said, "So my parents don't know I ran away with Bertie . . ."

As always, Ned chose his words carefully. "There are rumors. My perception is that your family is, to a certain extent, hoping that you *did* run off with someone, rather than that something more dire has happened to you. But nobody can figure how the princess fits into that scenario."

Imogene asked, "And the rumors about what happened to me?"

Ned shook his head. "No one thing. Abduction by an evil foreign power, or by magical beings, or by a love-crazed suitor . . ."

"That's just . . . ridiculous," Imogene said.

"Any more ridiculous than being a frog?" Ned asked. "How did that come to pass, anyway?"

Imogene saw no reason to hide what had happened, either from him or from Luella. "A frog told me he was a prince under an enchantment, and that I could return him to his true form by kissing him. What he didn't say was that the spell would switch over to me and make *me* a frog."

Ned said, "There are a couple of princes running around at the moment: your brother, Will, and someone named . . . Malcolm?"

"The son of some friends of my parents." Imogene had forgotten that King Calum and his family had been invited to participate in her birthday festivities.

Ned told her, "My impression was that both seemed genuinely worried about you. They passed by here early this morning, among the groups of people looking for you in the woods."

Imogene realized why Ned was sounding confused. "The frog wasn't either one of them. He wasn't a prince at all. Just a village boy." She turned to Luella. "Actually, a friend of your brother Tolf's: Harry."

"Harry?" Luella practically spat out the name. "Harry,

the wainwright's boy? That Harry? He's as big a nuisance as someone who ain't related to you *can* be." She paused as a thought came to her. "And, Imogene, he ain't even good-looking. I have to admit: You surprise me."

"I didn't kiss him because he's good-looking!" Imogene protested.

"No joking!" Luella scoffed.

"I kissed him because I thought that would be the end of the spell. I had no idea it would bounce back onto me."

Once more, it was Ned who brought them back around to the topic. "So, I'm guessing by the fact you're still a frog, lo this fortnight later, that this spell doesn't wear off. It needs to be . . . kissed off?"

Imogene grasped hold of the first part of what he'd said. Could the solution be as simple as that? "*Do* spells wear off?" she asked. It would be just like the old witch to have not known that—or to have forgotten to mention it.

Or, at least, Imogene liked to think so.

But Ned was shaking his head. "Don't know," he admitted. "I've had no personal experience with magic until now. I wrote a play, once, where time was the solution."

Imogene's patience snapped. "You also wrote a play with

a flying crow portrayed by a very non-flying frog." When Ned only shrugged, she said, "So you just made up the wearing-away thing? There's no reason to believe that will happen in this case?"

Ned said, "There are time frames that appear repeatedly in the old stories, which might be significant, or might mean nothing: One entire day. Three days. One week." Perhaps reluctant to be the bearer of bad news, he hesitated before adding, "A year."

"A *year*?" Imogene squealed, trying hard not to imagine this.

Ned broke eye contact before finishing, very quietly, "A hundred years."

Ever a faithful friend, Luella said, "Well, that's just wrong." But she didn't offer any reason behind that sentiment from which Imogene might take hope.

In the silence where they realized nobody had anything left to say, Imogene could now hear the distant voices of people in the woods that surrounded them. They were calling her name.

"Well," she said, "standing here gains us nothing. Luella, can you please bring me up to the castle? I'm hoping my father, or one of his advisors, can think of something." But she suspected this was wishful thinking.

Before Luella could move, Ned said, "You could wait for him there. Or you could wait for him here, which would be quicker." To Imogene's blank look, he explained, "I told you: *Everyone* is in the woods looking for you."

And a moment later, she realized that the voices were getting closer. One of the search parties was coming back in, either to refill their water skins at the stream or maybe to break for the evening meal.

When they emerged from between the trees, it turned out to be the group Prince Malcolm was leading. She recognized him immediately, even though it had been two years since she'd last seen him—when her family had done the traveling, to celebrate his eleventh birthday. *Wow!* she thought. He'd changed a lot in the interval between eleven and thirteen, having grown taller, with his face leaner and his body filled out nicely. She chided herself for noticing, asking herself, *What am I thinking? I'm not interested in boys.*

Well . . . not yet.

But if I was . . .

Luella, she thought, would approve of this one.

She even thought: *Good thing he's too young for her.*

But that was self-wounding nonsense. Because the circumstances were that she had changed more than he. And any change that involved turning green was *not* a change for the better.

She'd had time to think all that as twenty or so tired, mud-spattered, twig-bedecked people followed Prince Malcolm out of the woods. Two of them stopped short. The woman squealed, "Luella!" and then she and the man with her ran forward with their arms outstretched.

Realizing she was about to get squashed in a three-way hug, Imogene jumped in the only clear direction: from Luella's shoulder to Ned's.

Ned looked as startled by her decision as Imogene felt, but he stepped clear to give room to Luella and her family. Luella cried; her mother cried; her father blew his nose in a handkerchief and stared down at his feet as though this would prevent anyone from noticing that his eyes, too, were wet. Tolf was there also, though he'd hung back a bit. Now he gave Luella's upper arm a brotherly punch.

It was Prince Malcolm who cut things short. "Your daughter?" he asked, his voice already deepening into the tones of a man. But obviously he could already see that and was just using the question as a politeness, an excuse to step forward and intrude on a family's reuniting. He said to Luella, "Mistress Luella, we are all indeed delighted to see you safely returned to your family, and we look forward with eager anticipation to the chance to hear your story in great detail. But, first, I must ask: Any news of Princess Imogene?"

Oooh, nicely handled, Imogene thought, admiring the ease with which Malcolm took charge. *A natural king, that boy,* she thought. Had such ability come with *his* thirteenth birthday? At eleven, he'd been rather full of himself and somewhat irritating.

Luella started, "Ta—" then stopped short. Clearly, she had been too preoccupied to realize Imogene had jumped away. She turned her head to look at her right shoulder, where Imogene had been riding, and her face went white. "Nobody move!" she ordered, and she hurriedly searched the ground down among all the feet surrounding her.

Imogene cleared her froggy throat. "Here," she announced.

People hurriedly glanced all over the clearing before some finally settled on her.

"Ta-dah!" Luella said, although the moment had already lost some of its drama.

"Imogene?" a shaky voice asked.

A voice Imogene recognized as her mother's. Except her mother wasn't here, only these peasants with Prince Malcolm . . .

Ned's words came back to her. "Everyone," he had said. "*Everyone* is in the woods looking for you."

And only after all that did Imogene recognize the dirty, sweaty, tired-looking woman who stepped forward from the others. In her snagged and ripped dress, with no makeup, and her hair tied back, she had not one stitch of regality about her.

"Oh, Imogene!" her mother said, able—amongst all of them—to focus in on her daughter's voice, and to recognize it from one word, despite Imogene's improbable amphibian appearance. She cupped her hands and gently, gently—and not the slightest bit squeamishly—picked Imogene up off Ned's shoulder. "I am so glad you're safe," she said, which hardly seemed a reasonable comment, given Imogene's current condition.

But Imogene guessed that her mother had been imagining even worse.

And she herself was left with more feelings than words. In the end, she settled for "I'm sorry you were so worried."

"What happened?" her mother asked.

"Well," Imogene said, "I got turned into a frog."

"Yes . . . ?" her mother prompted. "How?"

Imogene noted that Harry was amongst the searchers. The sneaky, lying wretch. She saw him catch her looking at him, and his eyes darted back and forth as he no doubt weighed trying to slip off quietly against simply bolting. She considered telling the whole story but decided that the whole story, really, wouldn't gain her anything. The word Ned had used earlier came back to her. "Mischance," she said. "Magical mischance."

Luella's father said, "But what does that have to do . . . ?" His gaze bounced from Imogene to Luella and back. "Because her mother and I kind of thought Luella—"

His wife smacked his arm to keep him from announcing

to the world that they'd feared their daughter had run off with a man.

Tolf, Imogene noted, was looking hard at her, no doubt remembering the frog who had come to him for help, claiming to be a princess. Now he was about as green as a person who wasn't a frog could be.

"Luella," Imogene explained to everyone, "has been helping me and watching over me."

"Oh." Luella's father was obviously surprised. Luella's mother looked proud and pleased. Luella's brother looked dumbfounded. Then the father's gaze shifted to Ned. "So you . . . ?" he started. "You and Luella . . . ?"

"Never," Ned proclaimed, his hand over his heart as though shocked at the suggestion. "As beautiful as your daughter is—and she is *very* beautiful—as kindhearted and good . . . and innocent . . ."

Imogene remembered the context in which she'd last heard him use that word: as a substitute for *dimwitted.*

He shook his head. "I would never dishonor her that way."

"And so you are . . . ?" Luella's father persisted.

"A weary traveler," Ned said. "The three of us"—he indicated himself, Luella, and Imogene—"met here just moments ago."

Imogene *could* have said, *Yes, but not for the first time.* But she let it slide, because otherwise she'd have to betray Luella.

Her own mother brought the conversation back to Imogene's frogged state. "How do we turn you back to yourself?" she asked.

"Well . . ." Imogene said.

Once more, Prince Malcolm stepped forward. "Please pardon my boldness," he said, "but, from my reading, I do believe I know the solution, and—"

"No!" Imogene cried. "Back away!"

Startled, Prince Malcolm backed away.

"You don't understand," she told him. "If you kissed me . . ." She had the sudden uneasy worry that he might have had a different solution in mind, and that she had just needlessly embarrassed herself. But he nodded for her to go on. She sighed for all that she would miss in her life. Because, really, being a human had *so many* advantages over being a frog. She continued, "The spell doesn't end.

It just gets passed on." Then, to be sure that he—that all of them—understood, she finished, "If you kissed me, if anyone kissed me, then that person would become a frog in my place."

"All right," Prince Malcolm said. "Nonetheless . . ." Once more he stepped forward.

"What do you mean *nonetheless?*" Imogene demanded, ready to jump out of her mother's hands if that became necessary. "Didn't you hear what I just said?"

"It would have been hard not to," Malcolm pointed out, which Imogene guessed was his polite way of saying she was perhaps a bit louder than a perfectly proper princess should be. He, for one, was definitely much improved in manners since the last time they'd met, when he'd thought the funniest thing anyone could say was *underwear.* Now he said, "But that's what princes do: They help where they can, particularly where princesses are involved."

"Well, I'm sure that's very brave of you," Imogene said. And it *was* brave, she thought. Impressively so. The boy was sweet and brave as well as being good-looking. She continued, "But I wouldn't want the responsibility of knowing you were intentionally going to spend your life as a frog because of my carelessness." Well, it was really Harry's carelessness, but she had every intention of being a better person than Harry. Another thought came to her. "Or," she finished, "that you were planning on passing the spell on to some other unsuspecting soul."

Prince Malcolm did *not* put his hand to his heart, but all in all looked more sincere than Ned when he declared, "I would never do that. That would be wrong."

Luella suggested, "Maybe you could find someone who *wants* to be a frog."

And, while everyone looked at her with varying degrees of *Did she really say that?* astonishment, Imogene thought, *Who—besides a frog—would ever want to be a frog?*

The answer was *Nobody.*

And that, she saw, was the solution. "Luella! You are brilliant! We need a frog!"

"Luella ain't any kind of brilliant," Tolf pointed out. "We already got a frog. What we need is a princess."

It was Imogene's mother who caught on first. "Here," she said, and unceremoniously handed Imogene to Malcolm. "Don't drop her."

And with that, she hiked her skirts up as though totally

unmindful of her queenly dignity, and she waded into the stream.

"Quiet!" Imogene commanded.

The people all held very, very still.

And in the silence, Imogene could hear frogs croaking. And among all the croaks that she recognized as meaning "Food!" and "Dark's coming!" and . . . and, well mostly, "Food!" she heard the distinctive croak that she thought of as the "Hey, girls!" call.

"To your right," she directed her mother. "The far bank. Under that big leaf."

That particular frog's croaking had changed from "Hey, girls!" to the "Up!" warning, but luckily the creature decided to take its chances by staying still rather than by diving. Imogene's mother scooped him up in her bare hands as though holding frogs, even frogs who weren't her daughter, was something she'd always done. "Now what?" she asked.

"On the rock," Imogene said. In case the frog made a break for it, she didn't want him too close to the water.

Ned moved in to supply a steadying hand for the queen to use to haul herself up the bank of the stream, her shoes squishing with each step. She set the male frog down on the rock, then held her hands out, doing her best to keep him contained.

He could jump over your hands in a heartbeat, Imogene thought as Malcolm brought her closer. But the male frog had caught sight of her, and he stayed where he was.

Malcolm held her out, and Imogene puckered her little frog lips. Frogs are not really good kissers, but apparently this one was willing to give it a try.

Touching his lips was just about as much fun as kissing Harry had been. Once again she felt alternately fizzy and dizzy and topsy-turvy.

But after all of that, she also felt she had knees—who could have guessed one could be so nostalgic about having knees?—human knees that were pressing into the rock as she leaned over the frog, with Prince Malcolm's sure and steady hands at her waist, holding her from slipping. *Oooh, this is nice*, Imogene thought—a thought that covered a whole lot of things.

Princess Imogene Eustacia Wellington, who had come to suspect she was destined to spend the rest of her life as a frog, was once again human.

"Thank you," she said. To Malcolm, who continued to

hold her, for her human knees were wobbly. To her mother, who had understood her and quickly moved to do what was needed. To Luella, who had supplied the answer (even if she hadn't known it *was* the answer). To the townspeople, who were now cheering for her. To the old witch, in case she was listening. To the frog with whom she'd just exchanged a kiss.

The frog with whom she'd just exchanged a kiss hopped off the rock and back into the pond. Imogene hoped that, having been magically kissed into being twice the frog he'd been before, he'd be able to avoid getting eaten and would find the lady frog of his dreams.

While the crowd continued to cheer, the prince gave Imogene a kiss. "Sorry," he said, this time not at all sincerely, "I couldn't help myself." And Imogene liked it better than all of her previous kisses combined.

Her mother, between weeping and touching Imogene's hair so delicately and gingerly it almost seemed as though she was afraid Imogene would break, asked someone to please (*please*—her mother actually said *please!*) run ahead and ring the church bells to let the other search parties—especially the ones where her husband and her son were—know the good news as soon as possible. Only then did she hold Imogene out at arm's length and say, shaking her head, "Imogene, your dress."

Imogene glanced down at the dress she'd been wearing for the last two weeks—which gave every single appearance of having been worn for the last two weeks—and she took hold of her mother's arms and responded, "Yes, but, Mother, *your* dress."

For a moment, her mother looked shocked. But then she laughed.

And then they all headed up the hill toward the castle, with every one of the townsfolk invited to share in the birthday celebration turned into a *Hurray, we found the princess!* celebration.

Harry did have the good sense to slip away without joining them.

And the witch, of course, had never shown up.

Imogene heard Luella's father invite Ned to sit with them, apparently not having noticed that Ned was telling Luella all about how he was thinking of switching from plays to puppet shows, since puppets were less trouble than actors, and that oh by the way did she know that society had no constraints against female puppeteers?

Imogene watched Ned and Luella walk up the path arm in arm and thought, *Why not? Maybe – maybe I'm not such a bad princess, after all.* She went ahead and took hold of Malcolm's arm. "You," she told him with newfound boldness, "are a good person. Maybe a little reckless. But you have a good heart. I'm glad you're here."

"Thank you," he said. Then he smiled at her and added, "It helps to know what's expected in various situations. I have to admit I learned everything I know from this very helpful book called *The Art of Being a Prince*."

Which would have left Imogene speechless except that a princess is never at a loss for words. So she said, "That's very interesting."

And then Princess Imogene Eustacia Wellington twined her arm around Prince Malcolm's, and together they walked back to the castle.

Afterword

All the Best Princess Stories End "And Then They All Lived Happily Ever After"

(No argument there)

And then they all lived happily ever after.